Life With
Life Without

R. Troy Bridges

Illustrations by the Author

Bar Nothing Books
Adamant, Vermont

Photograph of Donaldson Prison by Joe Tew

Published in the United States by

Bar Nothing Books
351 Toby Hill Road
Adamant, VT 05640

Tel (802) 229–0691

info@barnothingbooks.com

publishing@barnothingbooks.com

SAN 256–615X

Printed in the United States

978–1-7378816–2-9 (softback)
978–1-7378816–3-6 (digital)

First Edition

Library of Congress Control Number: 2024951172

Preface

I suffered the typical childhood of a future criminal, complete with alcoholic and abusive parents, poverty and neglect. Surviving, I grew to be a man average in appearance and intelligence, but emotionally unstable.

I became a bank robber, although not a spectacular one; certainly not like the ones you read about or see in the movies. I didn't even use a gun. Barely disguised, I quietly walked into a bank, presented a note, and got the cash. Then, it was just a matter of walking out and calmly driving away. Sounds simple, doesn't it? Well, it was anything but. Any fool can walk into a bank, demand cash, and get it, but it's what happens after—the getaway—that's much more complicated.

Then, there's a third factor involved; one that precedes the other two, but is just as important. It's overcoming fear. Robbing a bank is a scary business. I thought about it for seven years before I found the courage ("courage" is probably not the right word; perhaps the phrase "the right state of mind" is more accurate) to actually rob a bank.

I found that right state of mind while stranded in Wichita, Kansas during the summer of 1986. There, sleeping in a stolen car that was almost out of gas, with less than a dollar in my pocket, dwelling on my past and the many mistakes I had made, seeing the world as hostile and vast, and myself as insignificant, I discovered that desperation equaled motivation and robbed my first bank.

I quickly squandered all the money I had stolen. Desperate again, I robbed another bank in Corpus Christi, Texas. Repeating this cycle over and over, I robbed 14 banks in seven different states during the next eighteen months. Then in September, 1987, I was hit by a car while making my getaway, ending my career as a bank robber and beginning my life as a prisoner.

But this is not a story about my bank robberies. I've already told that story (and about my earlier incarceration in federal prison and Angola state prison) in a recently published memoir entitled Spiral, a book that took me twenty years to write. And although the writing, editing, and rewriting of it was cathartic (forcing me to repeatedly revisit my childhood and life, and eventually helping me make peace with my past), I realized that to maintain continuity and focus on the message I wanted to convey, I would have to cut almost two-hundred pages. Much of that material was an outrageous story that I hadn't experienced directly, but had been told by a violent and colorful prisoner nicknamed Rooster. In expanding and retelling that story here, I imagined what some of the characters may have looked like, what they may have said, and even what they may have thought, all based on a composite of people I have known and the experiences I've had during my forty-six years spent in fifteen different prisons.

It's also the true story of an older prisoner I befriended named Jack. Jack's story, while not as violent, is equally memorable - and sadly, all too common in America's prisons.

This book is about friendship, loyalty, commonalities, and perseverance. Above all, it's about daring to hope while in an apparently hopeless situation.

The Characters

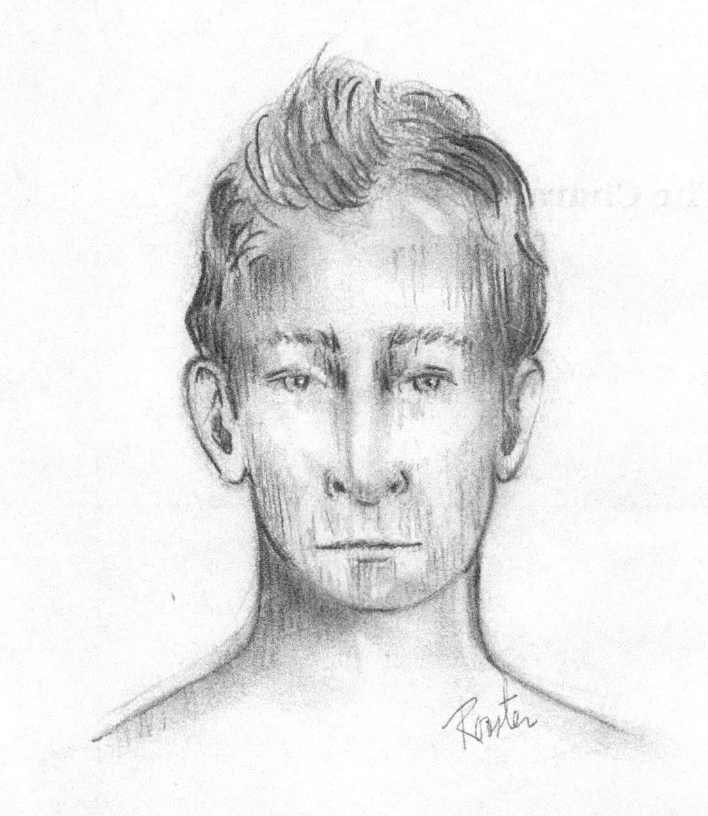

Rooster

Janice

Charlie

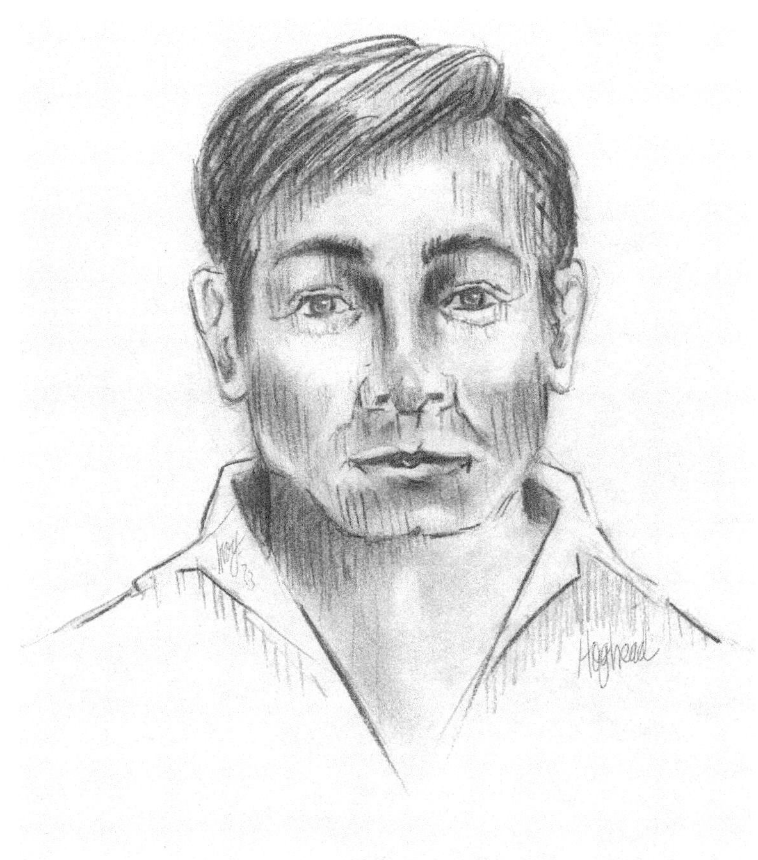

Hoghead

Jack

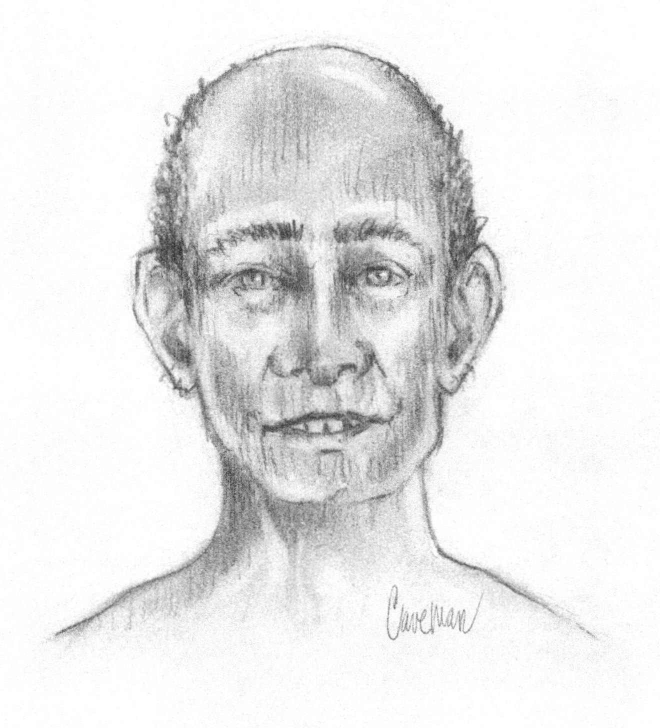

Caveman

Chapter One
The Doghouse

After a failed escape attempt in 1992, I found myself languishing in an isolation cell in Holman prison in South Alabama, serving three sentences for three separate bank robberies: life without parole in Alabama, an 18 year concurrent Federal sentence, and a 15 year consecutive Mississippi sentence.

Most, finding themselves in such a predicament would be depressed, maybe even suicidal, but not me. I had yet to abandon hope. I had grown up believing in the overused adage: "Where there's a will, there's a way" and was determined, as long as I had breath in my body and my mind was functioning well enough, to regain my freedom.

Then, one cold, rainy morning without notice, the warden, eager to rid himself of me and make me someone else's problem, had a guard escort me from my solitary confinement cell to a van parked near the back gate. When I asked where I was going, the guard said, "You'll find out when you get there. Just shut up and get in the van."

Carrying a laundry bag in hands cuffed to a chain wrapped around my waist, and walking carefully due to the leg-irons digging into my ankles, I climbed into the prison van. While attempting to sit down between two prisoners who had already claimed the window seats, I stepped on the foot of one of the men. "Excuse me," I mumbled. The man didn't answer; he just looked up, hatred in his eyes. Feeling uneasy and constrained, my left ankle throbbing, I carefully squeezed between the two men and sat down.

Cradling my laundry bag in my lap, I stared straight ahead and watched the rain spatter the windshield, waiting for the unknown and thinking, These damn leg irons are too tight. My left ankle hurts. It's always the left side. Sometimes I feel like I've been split down the middle. My right side still works pretty good, but my left has been through hell. I remembered when I broke my left ankle after jumping a fence while running from police in Mobile, and my left wrist in a bar fight in New Orleans. I winced inwardly when I recalled injuring my left knee while working on an oil rig in East Texas, and the partial deafness I suffered in my left ear after crashing through the windshield of a stolen car in Montgomery. And not once did I go to a doctor, I thought, 'cause doctors cost money and doctors ask questions. And one thing a man on the run can't afford is questions.

After a short while, the prisoner to my left, who obviously knew the prisoner to my right, leaned forward and spoke over me as if I was invisible. "I heard they're takin' us up North, probably to St. Clair or Donaldson."

"No shit," said the prisoner to my right. "I figured we might be goin' there. I just hope they drop me off at St. Clair prison, I sure as hell don't want nothin' to do with Donaldson; that place ain't nothin' but a throwaway camp."

"Yeah, they got all kinds of crazies up there," said the prisoner to my left. "My cousin did time there and you should hear the shit he told me about that place. You know it used to be called West Jefferson. That's where they built it, in West Jefferson County."

"Yeah, I heard that. Wonder why they changed the name."

"'Cause of that guard got killed up there a few years ago. You didn't hear about that?"

"Nah. How'd he get killed?"

"One of them crazies they had locked up in segregation killed 'im. He got into it with another dude, tried to stick 'im with this shank he made. The guard got in between 'em and got stabbed instead. Died on the spot, I heard. The guard's name was Donaldson, so they changed the name to Donaldson."

"Damn," said the prisoner to my right.

"Yeah, Donaldson's just one big fuckin' nuthouse. Ain't nothin' there but crazies and hard time."

Donaldson was a human warehouse where incarcerated men and women were dehumanized, abused, and afforded little opportunity for rehabilitation. It was freely called a "throwaway camp" by most prisoners. Some called it a perimeter prison.

Perimeter prisons, usually located in isolated areas far from public scrutiny, are generally populated by incorrigible and mentally-ill prisoners serving lengthy sentences. Most in Donaldson prison will never get out, and those few that do (usually after decades) often leave as illiterate and as angry as when they arrived, only to find that they've now been abandoned by families and friends. Having no job skills or money, and totally unprepared for life outside, most quickly reoffend.

Several factors helped create perimeter prisons. In the eighties, when funding was cut for the treatment of the mentally-ill and hundreds of treatment centers were shuttered, thousands of patients, untreated and unsupervised were released. Many were arrested, convicted and dumped into an already overcrowded prison system. There, misunderstood and mistreated by both inmate and prison personnel, many were raped, robbed, and beaten. Many more were locked inside punishment cells where they languished for years without medication or treatment.

Also during the eighties, some politicians' eager to be seen as tough on crime, passed the habitual offender law (also known as "Three Strikes and You're Out"), often resulting in habitual offenders being sentenced to life without parole for possession of a small amount of drugs or for stealing as little as a hundred dollars. Consequently, America's jails and prisons overflowed, prompting these same politicians to respond by building more prisons, often in rural areas with a high percentage of unemployment and a low percentage of registered voters. Dozens of new prisons sprang up, creating jobs for local workers and boosting local economies. Politicians touted this building boom as a win-win solution to the problems of unemployment in rural areas and prison overcrowding, but they failed to understand the long-term consequences of hiring undereducated, undertrained workers who were ill-prepared to deal with convicted felons (especially those suffering mental illness) and were biased, often having the same viewpoint of many in society: Prisoners are animals with no redeeming qualities. Just feed them and keep them under control, but more importantly, keep them inside the perimeter.

A couple hours later, parked outside the back gate to St. Clair prison, the prisoners to my left and right were told by the guard to grab their property and get out. "What about me?" I asked the guard.

"You! You stay," said the guard. "You're goin' to Donaldson."

Thirty minutes later, the van pulled inside the first of Donaldson's two back gates and parked to wait for the tower guard to open the second. After about ten minutes, the gate opened and we drove through and parked. The side door slid open and a guard holding a clipboard shouted, "Grab your property and get out."

Carrying my laundry bag, I stood on the blacktop and looked around, first up at the guard tower, then at the two, ten-foot fences topped with razor wire. That's when I noticed something I'd never seen before: Between the two tall fences was a third, shorter fence about eight feet tall. And attached to it was a small red-and-black sign with a lightning bolt painted on it. The sign read "Danger! Electric Fence." Looking closer, I saw that the fence was constructed of strands of electrical wire spaced about six inches apart. Attached to the wire were white ceramic insulators the size of softballs. Tangled in the wire near the bottom of the fence was a dead bird.

To my right was a large recreation yard the size of two football fields. Encircling it was a well-worn path. On the recreation yard was a volleyball net and a small area filled with weight benches and a mismatch of free weights. To my left was a softball field, complete with a backstop and small set of bleachers. Man, that don't look too bad, I thought. They got volleyball, weights, even a softball field. I can do time here.

Beyond the recreation yard and softball field were what looked like two steel barns (I later found out that these structures, originally intended for vocational training, had been converted into living areas because of overcrowding). Between the two structures were dozens of prisoners moving about; most seemed unconcerned, but several stood close to the back gate staring in the direction of the van, curious to see if the prisoner entering the back gate was a friend or foe.

The guard holding the clipboard ordered me to follow him. Walking in short, choppy steps, I followed him through the back gate, down a short blacktop, and into a large building. There, inside the prison's receiving area, the guard removed my handcuffs, belly chain, and leg irons. "Dump your gear there on the floor," he said.

After doing as I was told, I watched the guard search the contents of my laundry bag. When finished, he ordered me to strip. I removed my clothes, leaving them in a pile at my feet. The guard, now wearing gloves, said, "Turn around and face the wall. Bend over, squat, spread your butt cheeks, then cough."

Reluctantly I swallowed my embarrassment and did as I was told.

Satisfied, the guard said, "Okay, now stand up, turn around and face me. Lift your balls. Okay, now raise your arms. That's right; raise 'em high. Okay, now turn around and lift your feet. Let me see the bottoms."

Stumbling, I braced the wall with one hand and lifted my legs one at a time with the other.

"Okay," said the guard. He then carefully searched my clothes, dropping them onto the floor and sweeping them to the side with his foot. When finished, he signaled to a nearby trustee. The trustee came forward and dropped a t-shirt, boxer shorts, a white shirt and pants, a sheet, a blanket, and a torn, plastic mattress at my feet.

"Get dressed, put all your shit in your laundry bag, grab your mattress, and follow me," said the guard. He glanced at his clipboard. "I see here you got life without and you was in lockup at Holman. Also says you tried to escape."

"That's what they said, but they never charged me with it."

"That means I'm gonna have to put you in lockup here too. At least for ninety days. Besides, all new inmates comin' to Donaldson serving life without gotta do ninety days in Segregation."

"That don't make no sense, I ain't new. I been in prison in Alabama almost four years now. Spent a year in prison in Mississippi before that."

"Don't matter. You're new here, and they said you tried to escape. And on top of that you got life without, so you gotta go to lockup, you know, so we can observe you. See if you're suicidal or whatever. You don't kill yourself or nobody else, we'll let you out in population in about ninety days or so. Now hold out your hands and let me cuff you."

Prisoners at Donaldson called the segregation unit the doghouse. It was a hard and unforgiving place, too hot in summer (the heat index in the cells was often 120 degrees) and too cold in winter (with little heat and only one thin blanket for warmth).

In the doghouse, every morning at six a.m. two or more guards confiscated all the prisoners' mattresses, returning them at six p.m. And except for an hour outside three times a week (and a six-minute shower afterward), all were confined to their small, poorly-ventilated cells twenty-four hours a day. The menu, except for one day a month, seldom varied: Prisoners received two cold, unseasoned meals a day. Breakfast was at two-thirty (usually consisting of lumpy, congealed grits; thick, brown gravy with scum on top; a biscuit; and sometimes a spoon of powdered eggs), with supper twelve hours later (usually undercooked greens, cornbread, beans, and an unidentifiable meat patty).

Hands cuffed in front, I stuffed all my clothes in the laundry bag and threw the bag on top of the mattress. Grabbing a corner of the mattress, I dragged it behind me like a sled, following the guard down a short hall that emptied into a cavernous, two-story room lined with a tier of cells top and bottom. The first thing that struck me about the doghouse was the smell, and the second were the sounds. It smelled like a mixture of pine oil and unwashed bodies, and there was a constant buzzing, like the humming of a large generator, punctuated every so often by a loud shout or sharp howl.

Then I felt it like a slap in the face, not something seen or smelled or heard, but just as prevalent—tension. A tension so powerful it seemed to leap from cell to cell like static electricity on a dry day at high altitude. I was used to close confinement, harsh living conditions, and cold prison food, so the thought of living in a small cell for months on end didn't bother me, but what did bother me was the inescapable tension so pervasive in segregation units.

We stopped at a heavy, steel, grille gate, the number six crudely painted over the entrance. The guard said into his radio: "This is Taylor in receiving. Got one for you. Open Six Block." The grille gate slid open and I followed the guard through. He stopped in front of a cell marked 6-D-4. "Here," the guard said to me. "This is your new home." He smirked. Again he spoke into his radio: "Open cell four."

The heavy, steel door slid open with a loud clang of steel grinding against steel, jolting me head to foot; the sound caused me to wince and grit my teeth as if I'd suddenly been lashed with a whip. I paused at the entrance, closing my eyes. "Go on. Get in there," said the guard. "Don't gimme no trouble."

Just as I started through the door with my mattress, the guard said, "No, not your mattress. Just your laundry bag."

I paused again. "What, no mattress?"

"Nope. Not until six o'clock, then you'll get it back. Just leave it here in the hall. The trustee'll pick it up. Don't worry, you'll get it back at six."

"What kind of prison is this!" I exclaimed.

"It's the kind where you go to the doghouse; you don't get a mattress from six a.m. to six p.m.! You see, here at Donaldson we do things a little different."

"A lot different, you ask me," I said, rolling my eyes.

"Ain't nobody askin' you! Now grab your laundry bag and get your ass in there."

I entered the cell and dropped my laundry bag onto the concrete floor. The sliding door banged shut.

"Get up to the tray hole so I can get them cuffs off you," said the guard.

Stepping to the front of the cell, I lifted my hands to the narrow opening in the center of the barred door. The guard reached through and removed my handcuffs, then turned and walked away.

Rubbing my wrists, I looked around. The cell was small, not much larger than a walk-in closet. A concrete platform, measuring eighteen inches high by three feet wide stretched from the front to the back, taking up more than a third of the cell. On the back wall was a long, narrow window partially covered over with quarter-inch rusted, steel plating. Underneath the plating was a heavy, steel mesh screen so clogged with years of dust and grime that almost no sunlight or fresh air penetrated the cell. Positioned in the center of the back wall was a stainless steel toilet with a small sink above.

Digging into my laundry bag, I found a blanket and sheet, spread it on the concrete bed and lay down, using my laundry bag for a pillow. Squinting, I examined the uneven beads of steel some hapless prison worker had welded to attach the steel plating to the window frame. Impulsively, I counted the tiny holes in the steel mesh covering the narrow opening at the bottom of the window, eventually falling asleep.

A couple hours later, the door banged open, startling me awake. I sat up just as my mattress hit the floor with a dull thud. The door slammed shut. Getting up, I grabbed the mattress, flopped it onto the concrete slab, lay down and immediately fell asleep again.

Around two-thirty the next morning, I was awakened by the sound of a chow cart slowly creaking from cell to cell delivering breakfast. Getting up, I grabbed my food tray from the tray slot and, while sitting on my mattress, quickly ate the cold grits and brown gravy, wrapping the biscuit in toilet paper for later. After putting my empty tray in the tray slot, I slept again, only to be awakened at six when the cell door slid open again. Rolling over, I looked up to see a trustee and guard standing just outside my door. "What's up?" I asked.

"Your mattress, that's what's up," said the guard, his voice dripping sarcasm. "Throw it out."

Reluctantly, I flung my mattress into the narrow hall. The door slammed shut. I lay down on my concrete bed again and tried to go back to sleep again but couldn't get comfortable, so I got up and walked over to the sink. In its basin several roaches circled like skaters at a roller rink, their antennae waggling. Using my hand, I quickly swept the bugs out of the sink. They landed on the floor, righted themselves, then scattered in all directions. I stomped two with my bare feet before they could reach the safety of cracks in the concrete wall. Unrolling some toilet paper, I sat down on the toilet and wiped the bug guts from the bottom of my feet, then threw the toilet paper into the toilet bowl and flushed it.

After wiping the sink clean, I washed my face, then brushed my teeth while studying myself in the mirror and thinking about the events that had led to my present predicament. I remembered my childhood and many of the mistakes I'd made. I thought about all the years in prison that I was facing. Three bank robbery convictions in less than a year, I thought. Damn!

I felt a heavy pang of depression hit me, starting at the top of my head and slowly covering me like hot molasses. In the past, when such hopelessness overcame me, I would desperately try to find some distraction, usually drugs, or when I couldn't find or afford drugs, I would exercise, often working myself into exhaustion.

That worked temporarily. Then, by chance, one day a few years into my sentence, again in solitary confinement, I found a book that had been left in my cell by a former occupant. Up to that point I'd only read a handful of books, but with nothing else to distract me, I picked it up and started reading. The book, a Western, was easy to read, and I flew through the pages. Afterward, I felt something I hadn't in a long time—a sense of accomplishment. So I read the book a second time and then a third.

When released back into the general prison population, my first stop was the prison library. Over the next few years, as my skill and understanding improved, I graduated to more complex books on a wide range of subjects: religion, spirituality, physics, metaphysics, philosophy, psychology, and self-help.

I discovered that reading not only allowed me to mentally escape my physical prison (by transporting me to exotic locations and situations), but helped to ease the feelings of hopelessness and depression. And over time, reading became more than just a way to mitigate boredom, escape reality, or alleviate depression; it helped me change my perspective - helped me begin to challenge old, deeply-embedded beliefs and opened unexpected windows, windows that revealed new ways of seeing myself, others, and the world. Consequently, I began to rely on unhealthy addictions less and less. I continued to make poor decisions, just not as many and not as often.

For now, having nothing to read, I dropped to the floor and did push-ups until my arms trembled, then found the biscuit I had saved, ate it, and lay back down.

Chapter Two
The Walk

About fifteen minutes later, I heard the guard. "You wanna' walk?"

I opened my eyes, stood. "You mean go outside?"

"Yeah. Outside. Wanna walk?"

"Yeah."

"Well, come on then. Get dressed and get up here to this tray hole so I can cuff ya."

Handcuffed, I was led down the narrow hallway and through a heavy, steel door outside to a row of chain-link cages resembling a dog run. There, I was locked inside one of the small cages and my handcuffs removed.

"Be back in an hour," said the guard, looking at his watch.

I walked over, grabbed the fence, leaned my head back, closed my eyes, breathed in the sweet fresh air, and enjoyed the warmth of the early-morning sun on my face. A light breeze cooled my neck. I opened my eyes and in the distance I saw the guard tower near the front entrance and a portion of the parking lot. Beyond that, all I saw were thick woods. I turned and circled the cage. That's when I noticed another prisoner in the cage next to mine. He was doing push-ups on the concrete deck. Slim and red-haired, he appeared to be in his early-thirties. When he stood, we made eye contact. "You just get in the doghouse?" he asked, staring at me with intense, bright blue eyes.

"Yeah. Yesterday. You?" I asked.

"Nah, I been here awhile," he said. "What cell you in?"

"Cell four," I replied.

"That makes us neighbors. I'm in cell five. You gonna be a good neighbor or what?" asked the man, a slight grin on his face.

Surprised by his joking manner, I answered in kind, "Pretty good, I guess. You?"

"Yeah, I'm easy to get along with," he said. "Just joking, but the real reason I asked was because of that dude on the other side of you, cell three. He's called Sidewinder, and he ain't easy to get along with. That son of a bitch is a little wigged out, know what I mean?" He pointed to his head and made a circular motion with his forefinger. "Best to watch out when you pass his cell. He likes to throw piss and shit on anybody comes too close. Didn't take me long to figure out it's best to hug that outside wall when I walk past his cell, 'cause I don't need no more problems. That crazy fool splashes me I'm gonna fuck 'im up if I can get to 'im."

"I don't need no more problems either," I said. "What's wrong with 'im?"

"Done gone crazy, I guess. He's been in that same cell 'bout four or five years. Guess all that time cooped up in that small cell musta finally got to him."

"Thanks for the heads up," I said.

"No problem. They call me Rooster."

"Name's Troy," I said. "Where'd you get a nickname like Rooster?"

"That ain't hard to figure out, just look at my hair. Sticks up like a rooster. They been callin' me that since I was a kid. How long you got in the doghouse?" he asked.

"Ninety days. Least that's what they told me in Receiving, said that because I was in lockup at Holman and got life without, they gotta' observe me, see if I'm gonna' try to kill myself or whatever."

"Yeah, I got life without too, for a robbery outta Mobile. And seems to me like them bastards been observin' me for the last seven years."

"You been in the doghouse seven years!"

"Nah, not seven years. I spent most of my time in population, but I been in the doghouse about thirteen months now. Only got five more to go."

"Damn, that's eighteen months. You don't mind me askin', why'd you get so much time in the doghouse?"

"Nah, it don't bother me," said Rooster. "You see, I got into it with this dude owed me money, and he didn't wanna pay. And he disrespected me. It's a long story."

"Hey, I got at least ninety days," I joked.

"Well, it ain't that long," smiled Rooster, stepping closer to the fence that separated us. Then, as if reliving a memory, Rooster's face changed. He was silent for a moment, then said, "Well, I guess it all kinda started with Janice, Charlie's wife. Charlie's the dude I used to run with. But, he's dead now. Anyway, it started with Janice. I mean, she wasn't the cause of what happened, but she was the one brought us the dope, so I guess it all started with her. I saw her a couple of times on the visitin' yard when she came to visit Charlie, but that was before my mama passed away. Anyway, I don't visit no more. She was a tall, skinny girl, kinda pretty, and she was good to Charlie. She came to see him about twice a month, usually brought a little dope with her."

I stepped closer to the fence, held on, head down, and listened while Rooster began to tell me how he ended up in the doghouse.

Chapter Three
The Visit

Janice was tall and thin. She had long, blonde hair and was often described as nice-looking. Married the first time at seventeen, she had given birth to three children by three different men by the time she and Charlie had met and married.

Janice had little formal education and had lived a hard life, but somehow had managed to maintain a positive outlook and a sweet disposition. She was a hard worker, a loving, attentive mother, and was devoted to Charlie, who she had married three years earlier. A year into their marriage, Charlie was arrested, convicted and sent to prison.

Janice visited Charlie every two weeks. And often, before she left her rented mobile home for the drive to Donaldson prison, she compressed an ounce of marijuana and thirty Valium into a tight roll the size of a fat cigar, wrapped it with electrical tape, and put it in her purse.

The drive to Donaldson took about an hour. Ten miles from the prison, Janice pulled into a rest area, went into the public restroom, and closed and locked the door. Pulling her pants to her knees, she sat on the toilet seat, reached into her purse and removed the cigar-shaped package. Holding it in her hand, she looked at it with fear and disgust, then reached down and carefully inserted the package in her vagina. Standing, she straightened her clothes and left the stall.

Meanwhile, Charlie sat on the toilet and plunged his forefinger into a jar of Vaseline. He inserted his finger into his rectum, evenly spreading the lubricant, then stood, pulled up his pants and walked over to a bank of sinks. There, while washing his hands he turned first to the right, then to the left, admiring his reflection in the stainless steel mirror mounted on the wall.

In his early-thirties and already serving life without parole for burglarizing a drug store, Charlie stood five-ten and was slim and muscular. Handsome as a movie star, he had dark black hair and chiseled features, but hard, gray eyes. Simple-minded and angry most of the time, Charlie was pleasant only when he was stoned, a pursuit to which he devoted most of his time, energy and resources.

"Might wanna shake a leg," said Hoghead, walking up behind Charlie. "They just called your name for a visit over the loudspeaker."

Hoghead was a large man. He stood six-three and weighed over three hundred pounds. Average in intelligence, he had a good sense of humor and loved a good prank, often making Charlie the butt of his jokes. But Hoghead could also be serious, and even cruel when he felt that he had been taken advantage of.

"I heard 'em," said Charlie. "Ain't no rush. I'll get there when I get there. I don't need nobody babysittin' me."

"Charlie, that's exactly what your dumbass needs...a babysitter," said Hoghead.

"And what you need is one of them dog muzzles on that big mouth of yours. 'Course I doubt they could find one big enough to fit that watermelon head you got."

"Fuck you!" said Hoghead, walking away.

"And fuck you!" yelled Charlie, continuing to comb his hair and admire his reflection in the mirror.

Satisfied, Charlie left the toilet area and walked past Hoghead and Rooster, who were sitting on Rooster's bunk drinking coffee. "I'm outta here," said Charlie.

"'Bout time," said Hoghead. "That wife of yours ain't gonna wait forever."

"She'll wait as long as it takes," said Charlie. "I'm the best thing she ever had."

"You just keep believin' that shit," said Hoghead, "and one of the days she's gonna dump your stupid ass."

"Ain't gonna happen," said Charlie, continuing toward the exit. "Ain't never gonna happen," he repeated, walking through the door.

"See you when you get back," yelled Rooster at Charlie's back.

Rooster was a riddle. Clearly the most intelligent of the three, and the smallest, he was also the most bitter and the most dangerous. Standing five-six and weighing only a hundred-thirty-five pounds, Rooster wasn't handsome like Charlie, but he was presentable, with average features, reddish-orange hair, and a vicious stare. Rooster's mood could change quickly. He could be kind and tolerant one moment and cruel and unforgiving the next. A volatile child of the streets of Mobile, he grew to maturity in reform school and finally prison. Accordingly, Rooster was a planner and thinker, and during his seven years at Donaldson had developed a reputation as a hard, dangerous man. Rooster was the type of man that other prisoners secretly pointed to and remarked, "You see that little, red-haired dude over there. That's Rooster. I know he don't look like much, but don't let that fool ya'. He ain't nothin' to play with. No siree, he ain't nothin' to fuck with."

Rooster paused. He turned, and for a moment stared at the woods beyond the fences, remembering Janice. He then turned back, grabbed the fence that separated us, looked me in the eyes and continued.

Janice was early and the prison parking lot almost empty. After parking her battered, old Chevrolet near the entrance she turned off the ignition, then on impulse turned the key to restart it. The ignition clicked twice, then reluctantly restarted. Janice quickly turned it off. Frustrated, she thought, It's gettin' harder and harder to start. One of these days it ain't gonna start at all. I just know it. Then what? How am I gonna get to work, get the kids to school? I told Charlie I needed money to get this damn car fixed, but he just won't listen.

Janice reached into her purse, removed her driver's license and a small, clear, plastic pouch full of change she would spend in the prison's vending machines. She then grabbed her car keys, put them in the plastic pouch, locked the car and left. As she walked across the parking lot toward the prison's reception center, she felt the drug package move inside her. Pausing, she took a deep breath, swallowed her fear, then continued moving toward the center, just outside the prison's ten-foot perimeter fences.

Inside, Janice was met by a female guard who asked to see her driver's license, then asked the name of the prisoner she was there to visit. Janice nervously tapped her foot while waiting for the guard to search a computer on the counter that separated them. Finally, the guard said, "Okay, you're on the approved list. Wait here and I'll get somebody to take you to the restroom."

A few minutes later, a second female guard escorted Janice to a nearby restroom. "Lift your bra and turn the cups inside out," the guard told Janice. Janice did as she was told without complaint. "Okay, now unbutton your pants and unzip them." Again, Janice calmly complied. Assured that Janice was wearing underwear, the guard patiently waited until Janice straightened her clothes then pat-searched her. "Okay, you're good to go," said the guard. "Have a nice visit."

After leaving the reception center, Janice stepped outside to stand at the base of a tall guard tower. She patiently waited for the guard in the tower to electronically open the first gate. While waiting she heard what sounded like the tinkling of a wind chime overhead and looked up, momentarily blinded by the glare of the early-morning sun. She shielded her eyes with her hand and saw that it was only a stiff breeze shaking the coils of razor wire atop the tall fences. Transfixed by the sound, she stared at the razor wire for a moment, then turned her attention to the electronic gate, willing it to open. A few moments later the gate buzzed an alarm and the gate popped open. Janice walked through and the gate slammed shut, leaving Janice in a no-man's land between two fences. Feeling trapped, she looked up at the tower, again willing the guard to quickly open the second gate, and in less than a minute he did. Janice hurried through, then followed the sidewalk that led to the prison's entrance fifty yards away. Opening a heavy glass door, she stepped into a foyer with a high ceiling, crossed it, opened another glass door and entered the prison's visitation area.

Charlie left the dorm and walked down a long hall until he reached the prison's control center. There, he looked through thick Plexiglas to see a guard sitting inside. Leaning into a speaker, Charlie asked, "You call me for a visit?"

"Yeah, you got a visit," said the guard, recognizing Charlie as one of the few inmates who visited regularly. He was also aware that Charlie was listed on a "hot-sheet" of known drug users, and remembered that during an earlier briefing he had been told by his supervisor to watch Charlie closely when he visited.

"Okay," said the guard, pushing a button to open an electronic grille gate. "Go on through."

Charlie walked through the grille gate, then down a short hall, opened a door and entered the inmate dressing room. There, he was met by Officer Beaumont, the senior guard in charge of visitation. He too had been told to watch Charlie closely.

"What size jumpsuit you want, Charlie?" asked the guard.

"Better gimme' an extra-large," said Charlie. "These damn jumpsuits ride up on ya, you know, and I need all the extra room I can get. Gotta protect the old family jewels, know what I mean?" He laughed.

Officer Beaumont didn't respond. Instead, he turned to an inmate worker standing in a small room lined with wooden cubicles stuffed with bright, orange jumpsuits. "Give him an extra-large," he told the worker.

Charlie quickly removed his everyday prison whites, rolled them into a ball, and passed them through a small window to the worker, who in turn handed Charlie a jumpsuit.

After dressing, Charlie walked through a final door and into the prison's visiting area. He stood for a moment and looked around. It was a large room with a tall ceiling; the walls were painted beige. One long wall was lined with vending machines and had several small tables with microwave ovens setting on them. Half of the back wall was taken up by the prison's small post office (now shuttered), and the other half by two restrooms for the visitors' use. Neat rows of small tables and plastic chairs filled the rest of the room. Surveillance cameras, monitored by a guard in the control center, were strategically placed throughout. Charlie walked over to his usual table near the vending machines and sat down.

Walking into the visitation room, Janice looked around and spotted Charlie sitting at their usual table. When Charlie saw her, he smiled and stood. They met in the center of the room, embraced, kissed, then walked hand in hand to the table and sat down.

"Did you bring the package?" whispered Charlie.

"Don't I always!" said Janice, an edge to her voice.

"Yeah, baby, yeah," said Charlie, sensing her irritation. He quickly changed the subject. "How're the kids?"

"They're okay," said Janice, momentarily soothed. "I dropped them off at Mother's. But Lucy's still gotta cold. I gave here some children's Tylenol last night. She had a fever, but it was down this mornin'. The other two are okay. Growin' like weeds."

"Listen," interrupted Charlie, looking around the room. "Wait and gimme' the package when it gets more crowded, just like last time."

"Okay, Charlie," said Janice, squeezing Charlie's arm, forcing him to look her in the eyes, well aware that she would have his full attention for only a minute. "Charlie. How long I gotta keep doin' this? It scares me, and I know we're gonna get caught sooner or later."

"Shit, Jan, we ain't gonna get caught. These bastards couldn't catch a cold they was naked in the North Pole. Anyway, it won't be much longer. Just 'til we get ahead. You know we need the extra money. They ain't payin' you shit at that job you got.

And I told you I can get fifty dollars a matchbox for weed in here."

"But, that's just it, Charlie. You ain't sendin' me hardly nothin' now. How we gonna get ahead? And suppose we get caught? What's gonna happen to the kids?"

"Ain't my fault I couldn't send you more money last time!"

"And the time before that, and the time before that!" said Janice.

"A couple guys ain't paid me yet. When they do, I'll send you some extra."

"I'm tellin' you, it just ain't worth it. Right now I'm behind on my rent and can't hardly put food on the table, much less keep gas in the car. And that's another thing, Charlie. My car's 'bout to break down on me. Right now when I try to start it, sometimes all it does is make a clickin' sound."

"Shit, that's probably just the bushins' worn out on the solenoid. Man, if I was out I'd have that thing fixed in thirty minutes."

"But that's the point Charlie, you ain't out, and I'm out here by myself with no help, and I'm the one gotta deal with all this. And I'm tellin' you, Charlie, we're gonna get caught we keep doin' it. I know it. Then what!"

"Look, soon as I sell the pot this time I'm gonna' send you some extra—enough to get the car fixed. How's that sound?"

"Sounds good if you'll do it, and we don't get caught", said Janice. "Last time you promised me you was gonna send me two-fifty and all I got was a hundred. I didn't even have enough money to buy the pot - had to use some of my rent money."

"Jan, you worry too much."

"And you don't worry enough!" said Janice. "You know we got kids to feed and bills to pay!"

"Look, baby, I give you my word that when I box up the shit this time, I'm gonna sell six matchboxes off the top, before I even smoke a joint, and then I'm gonna send you three-hundred." Charlie reached across the table and caressed Janice's hands. Her eyes softened. "Okay?" whispered Charlie.

"Okay, Charlie," sighed Janice, not pacified, but tired, simply giving up, having heard his empty promises before.

"Let's get somethin' to eat," said Charlie.

Chapter Four
The Hole in the Wall

"Let's go. Time's up!," shouted the guard, interrupting Rooster. He then turned to me. "I'll be back to get you in about ten minutes."

"Damn," said Rooster to me. "I'll finish this when we get back inside!"

"How you gonna do that? I asked.

"You'll see," replied Rooster over his shoulder as he was escorted from the cage.

Knowing that the doghouse was purposely constructed to prevent communication between cells, I wondered just how Rooster intended to finish telling me his story.

Fifteen minutes later, back in my cell, I heard a dull thumping sound coming from the concrete wall that separated my cell from Rooster's, then a faint voice, as if coming from far away. "Hey," the voice said. "Hey, Troy, look up. See that hole in the wall right above your head. You see it?"

I looked up. "What hole!" I yelled back.

"That hole right above your head," said the muffled voice.

I climbed onto the concrete bed and searched until I found a hole chest-high and about an inch in diameter. It was stuffed with a wad of toilet paper. "I see it!" It's got toilet paper stuck in it!" I yelled into the wall.

"Dig it out!" shouted Rooster.

"Just a minute." I jumped down, stepped over to the sink and picked up my toothbrush. Using the handle, I removed the toilet paper, then looked through the hole. Startled by the eye staring back at me, I jumped back. "What the hell!" I laughed.

"I see youuu!" shouted Rooster. "Put your ear to the hole so I can hear you." I leaned the right side of my head against the wall and clearly heard, "See. We got us a telephone. How 'bout that!"

"You gotta be kiddin' me," I said into the hole. "You dig this hole?

"Nah, it was here when I got here. One day I noticed this hole stuffed with toilet paper and dug it out. That's when I saw that the hole went all the way through to the other side, so I yelled at my partner Charlie, just like I did you."

"The same Charlie that's in the story you was tellin' me when we were outside?"

"Yeah, that Charlie. When they locked us up, he was in the cell you're in now."

"What happened to him?"

"Remember I told you he died."

"Oh yeah, that's right."

"Well anyway, he was in the same cell you're in now. Sometimes we'd talk all night. We used to have some helluva conversations." There was an uneasy silence for a short time, then Rooster said, "Look, whenever you wanna talk, all you gotta do is beat on the wall a couple times. And when you want some privacy, just keep it plugged up."

"Alright," I said. "You was tellin' me about Charlie and Janice visitin'."

"Oh yeah," said Rooster through the hole. He continued the story.

Two hours later, the visitation area now filled with prisoners, their friends, and families, Charlie said to Janice, "Now's a good time to pass it to me, while them guards is busy."

Janice reached down and carefully pulled open the Velcro closure she had sewn into the crotch of her jeans. With two fingers she reached in and slipped her panties to the side. Janice squeezed her pelvic muscles and expelled the dope package into her hand. She looked over at Charlie and nodded her head. Charlie reached under the table and Janice passed the package to him.

Janice resealed the crotch of her jeans, then reached over and picked up a bag of popcorn sitting on the table. Grabbing a handful, she passed the bag to Charlie. He reached in the bag, dropped the dope package inside, then came out with a handful himself. Charlie smiled. "Let's get a Coke," he said.

Hand in hand, they walked over to the bank of vending machines. There, Janice got a soda, opened it and took a long drink. Charlie stood beside her, scanning the room, but oblivious to the newly installed surveillance cameras. "Move over in front of me," Charlie told Janice, taking a step back to stand between two vending machines, his back to the wall. Holding the bag of popcorn in his left hand, he reached down with his right and unbuttoned the fly on his jumpsuit. He then reached into the bag of popcorn, palmed the tightly-bound drug package, bent his knees, leaned forward and passed it between his legs. Relaxing his sphincter muscles, Charlie slipped the tip of the cigar-shaped package into his rectum. Willing himself to relax again, he gave a final push and the package disappeared inside. He buttoned his fly, smiled at Janice and said, "Let's go sit down."

Once they were seated, Charlie said, "See, I told you weren't nothin' to worry about. All it takes is a little plannin'."

"I still don't like it," said Janice.

"I told you, you worry too much."

A few minutes later, Officer Beaumont walked up to Charlie. "I need you to come with me," he said.

"What's up?" I ain't finished my visit yet."

"Just come with me and I'll tell you," insisted the guard.

"Damn!" said Charlie, standing. "A man can't even visit with his wife without being harassed!" He kicked the chair in frustration.

"Let's go, Charlie," said Officer Beaumont. "Now!"

Charlie put his hand on Janice's shoulder. "It's okay," he reassured her. "I'll be right back."

Chapter Five
Sidewinder

"Shower! shouted a guard, interrupting Rooster again. "Get ready to shower!"

"Shower time, "Rooster said through the hole in the wall. "I'll have to finish this later. Look, let me hip you to somethin'. if you ain't standin' at your door waitin' when that asshole guard gets to your cell, he'll pass you up and go on to the next cell. So be ready if you don't wanna miss your shower."

I plugged the hole in the wall, stripped down to my underwear, and was sitting on the concrete bed awaiting my turn in the shower when I heard the guard shout, "Cell three, you wanna shower!" then, "Sidewinder! You gonna shower or what!" After a short pause, I heard the guard tell Sidewinder, "Okay, that's your choice you don't wanna shower your nasty ass."

A moment later, the guard stood in front of my cell door. "Cell four, you wanna shower?"

"Sure do," I said.

"Well, come on. Get up here so I can cuff you."

Wearing only boxer shorts, and holding a towel, washcloth, and a bar of soap, I lifted my hands to the tray slot and the guard handcuffed me. He then escorted me down the hall to a large shower stall. When we walked past cell three Sidewinder yelled, "Hey, you fuckin' pig, you skipped me!"

That's when I got my first look at the man nicknamed Sidewinder. He was tall, skinny and pasty white. His dark eyes were wild and unfocused. He had long, fuzzy, matted blonde hair. Totally naked, he stood at the front of the cell, holding onto the bars while rocking his body back and forth.

"Sidewinder," said the guard. "I done asked your crazy ass twice if you wanted a shower and you didn't answer. Now, it's too late, 'cause that train done left the station. So go lay down. I don't wanna hear no more shit outta ya. And for God's sake, put on some fuckin' clothes! Ain't nobody wants to look at your naked ass!"

"I want my fuckin' shower, you bastard! You skipped me! I want my shower!"

"Too bad!" yelled the guard, motioning for me to keep walking.

At the shower stall, the guard removed my handcuffs. "You got six minutes," he said, looking at his wristwatch. He stepped to the side and lit a cigarette.

I stepped into the shower stall, quickly adjusted the water temperature, then soaped my body. I scrubbed, rinsed, then stood still, letting the hot water massage me.

"Time's up!" shouted the guard, stomping his cigarette out. "Let's go! I got twenty more convicts to shower!"

Wrapping my towel around my waist, I grabbed my soap and washcloth and stepped from the shower stall. The guard handcuffed me and we headed back down the catwalk. When we came near cell three again, I cautiously hugged the far wall just as Rooster had advised, and was glad later that I had heeded his advice, because just as we reached Sidewinder's cell, his arm flashed through the tray hole, and in it was a Styrofoam cup of urine. The urine splashed the guard in the upper back, soaking his shirt and pants and causing him to stop and hunch his shoulders, as if someone had dumped a bucket of ice on him. His face filled with rage. He spun and charged Sidewinder's cell, slamming the the tray slot with his baton, barely missing Sidewinder's outstretched arm.

"You fuckin' crazy bastard!" yelled the guard. "You're gonna pay big time for this!"

"Ha! Ha!" laughed Sidewinder. "I got you! I told you I needed my shower! Got your ass good!"

"You gonna get somethin', alright! But it ain't gonna be no shower!"

The guard, reeking of urine, quickly locked me in my cell, then rushed off toward the cubicle.

I hung my towel and washcloth to dry, then pounded on the wall. "Hey, Rooster!" I shouted. "Rooster."

"Yeah," said Rooster into the hole. "What's up?"

"You ain't gonna believe it."

"Believe what?"

"Well, it might be awhile before you shower. When I was comin' back from the shower just now,

Sidewinder splashed the guard with a cup of piss. I'm tellin" you, that guard was hot as a firecracker. You shoulda seen his face."

"I told ya! What'd I tell you!" yelled Rooster. "I told ya that crazy bastard would throw piss on you! Did he get you, too?"

"Nah, I was walking close to the wall like you said, but he got that guard good."

"Watch what happens," said Rooster. "Any minute now the goon squad'll be down here. Just watch what I tell you. They're gonna bust up in here and kick Sidewinder's ass. Happens every time he splashes one of 'em. I can't tell you the number of times I've heard 'em kickin' his ass. But you know what?"

"What?"

"Sidewinder don't give a fuck, not really. I think he likes to get his ass kicked every so often. Might be what they call masodicked. You know, gets a kick outta gettin' beat up. Man, I tell you, that's one weird dude."

"No doubt, Sidewinder's got a lot of mental problems me and you don't know nothin' about. I read once in this book that sometimes when you keep a man isolated with no human contact, he'll act out just to get the contact he craves, you know, just to get that human touch, even if that touch gets him beat up instead of hugged. Sidewinder don't need his ass kicked; what he needs is a psychiatrist."

"Oh, they fixin' to give him a hug, alright. They fixin' to give him what they call a serious attitude adjustment," said Rooster.

"I'm gonna go lay down," I said.

"Holler at you later," said Rooster, plugging the hole in the wall.

Ten minutes later I heard the static of a two-way radio, got up and walked to the front of my cell. Leaning my head against the steel bars, I saw three members of the Correctional Emergency Response Team standing beside a gurney stationed just outside Sidewinder's cell. Dressed in black, they each wore padded vests, helmets with plastic face guards, and carried large, Plexiglas shields, long nightsticks, and canisters of pepper spray.

Sidewinder, defiant, also waited, and he too was prepared. Now fully dressed, his pants and shirt stuffed with cotton torn from his mattress, he looked like the Michelin man. On his head he wore a helmet fashioned out of a small cardboard box, and in his hand he held a sock with two bars of soap in it.

The lead guard yelled, "Open cell three!" When the door slid open, the three guards rushed inside and formed a wedge with their shields. They advanced on Sidewinder, who had backed into a corner of his cell.

"Come on, you bastards!" slobbered Side- winder, swinging his sock and soap weapon in a circular motion.

The tactical team advanced and Sidewinder swung his sock weapon like a flail. It bounced off the lead guard's shield and Sidewinder dropped it. Sidewinder then punched and kicked at the shield with his feet and fists, but did no harm. The first guard to reach Sidewinder easily pinned him against the wall. The second guard sprayed Sidewinder with pepper spray, and the third kicked his feet from under him. Sidewinder crumpled to the floor, and the lead guard kicked him in the head, crumpling Sidewinder's cardboard helmet.

Handcuffed, yelling and screaming, Sidewinder was dragged from the cell like a side of beef and dumped into the hall. He was forcibly strapped to the gurney and taken to a padded cell in the infirmary.

Later that day, I asked Rooster, "What ya think they'll do to Sidewinder?"

"Not too much. They'll probably fill his ass full of Thorazine or somethin', keep him in a padded cell for a week or so, then send him back. Like I told you, this ain't the first time he's throwed piss on one of them guards. Seems Sidewinder ain't never gonna learn to quit fuckin' with these folks."

"Rooster, I don't know much about what makes Sidewinder tick, but from what I've read - and that's just a couple books on psychology - and I barely understood most of it - I doubt he can learn to quit fuckin' with 'em, not without some professional help, anyway."

"He ain't hittin' on all eight cylinders, that's for sure," said Rooster, "but he sure as hell ain't gonna get help here at Donaldson. Well, since I got you up here at the hole, I'll finish tellin' you what happened to Janice and Charlie,"

"Alright."

"Well, after the visitation guard took Charlie back to the dressin' room, he searched him real good," said Rooster.

"Did they find the dope?"

"Just hold your horses," said Rooster, "and I'll tell ya."

Chapter Six
The Bucket

Officer Beaumont escorted Charlie to the dressing room. There, he told him, "Strip naked."

"What's this shit all about!" shouted Charlie. "I ain't even finished my visit yet."

"Oh, you're finished, alright," said the guard. "Just keep quiet and do what I tell you. Now strip!"

Charlie reluctantly removed his clothes and dropped them in a pile at Officer Beaumont's feet. The guard stretched a pair of rubber gloves over his hands, then piece by piece thoroughly searched Charlie's jumpsuit and underwear.

"Now turn around, bend over, and spread your ass cheeks. You know the routine."

"Man, this is bullshit!" protested Charlie, but he did as he was told.

"What's that up your ass? Looks like grease to me. You got some dope stuck up your ass, Charlie?"

Charlie straightened. He turned and faced the guard. "I don't know what the fuck you're trippin' on Beaumont! That ain't nothin' but hemorrhoid medicine! I got problems with hemorrhoids."

"Right, Charlie. You can tell me just about anything and I'll believe it. I'll tell you what - you got a problem alright, but it ain't hemorrhoids. Put your clothes on. I'm takin' you to see the captain."

"The captain! For what! I ain't even finished my visit yet. I still got an hour and a half left."

"Your visit's been terminated. Now put your clothes on like I told you."

"Can't I at least tell my wife goodbye?"

"No! We'll tell her goodbye for 'ya. Your visit's over."

"This is pure-d harassment, that's what it is! Damn right I wanna see the captain! I wanna get some straightenin'. And I'm gonna tell him about all the bullshit a man's gotta go through just to visit with his wife. Damn right, I wanna see the captain!"

Officer Beaumont handcuffed Charlie and escorted him to the captain's office.

Captain Rankhart was a short, barrel-chested man in his late-forties. His father had worked at Donaldson when it first opened in the eighties, and after a short stint in the Army, Rankhart had followed in his father's footsteps, working his way up through the ranks.

In his office, Captain Rankhart, after hearing what Officer Beaumont told him in private, said to Charlie, "Charlie, I got reason to believe you're smugglin' drugs into my prison and I ain't gonna put up with it."

"Captain, I ain't."

"Just stop right there," said Rankhart, holding up his hand to silence Charlie. "Hold it right there before you say anything else and listen to me. One of my officers watchin' the cameras saw you put somethin' down the front of your jumpsuit while you was standin' at the vendin' machines."

"That's bullshit, Captain! What he saw was me scratchin' my ass!" He then turned to look at Officer Beaumont. "I told Beaumont here I got hemorrhoid problems and that's the truth."

"Oh, don't worry Charlile, we're gonna get to the truth. You can believe that!" Deciding to try a softer approach, Rankhart calmly continued. "Look, Charlie. Why don't you just come clean, give us the drugs, and make it easier on everybody. Save everybody, includin' yourself, a lot of trouble. We know for a fact you been smugglin' drugs."

"I ain't got no drugs, Captain," said Charlie.

"Well, okay Charlie, if that's the way you want to play it," said Rankhart. "I'll tell you what we're gonna do then. I'm gonna lock you up in the infirmary holdin' cell and I'm gonna' put an officer and a bucket in there with you. And you're gonna stay in that holdin' ccll 'til you shit in that bucket. And when you do, if we find drugs, you'll be charged with possession, and also charged with introducin' drugs into a state facility, and you're gonna get more time. That's not all, Charlie. If we find drugs, and you know we're gonna find 'em, we'll charge your wife too. Give her some time. You want that?"

"I ain't got no dope, Captain."

"Come on, Charlie. This is your last chance to make it easier on yourself, and maybe your wife too. What's it gonna be?"

Charlie didn't answer.

"Okay, then," said Rankhart, throwing up his hands. "That's it. You've had your chance." He turned to the officer. "Beaumont, get on the radio and tell Officer Davis that I need him to come to my office and get this man, take him to the infirmary holdin' cell. And tell him to bring some duct tape, toilet paper, and a five-gallon bucket. Now cuff this man's hands behind him, and don't let 'im outta your sight 'til Davis gets here."

Officer Davis had been a farmer all his life, but when his cotton crop was destroyed by a hurricane ten years earlier, he found a crop not dependent on the weather, one much hardier and always in demand. With the help of his brother-in-law, who worked at Donaldson—and despite having only a third grade education—he enrolled in a short training program and was hired as a guard at the prison.

A tall, slim, red-faced man, Officer Davis could barely read or write (and was assigned the jobs most officers avoided), handcuffed Charlie's hands in front, then wrapped duct tape around the cuffs of Charlie's pants.

"Why you wrappin' the bottom of my pants with tape?" asked Charlie.

"Well now Charlie, we wouldn't want you shittin' that dope package down your pants leg while I ain't lookin', now would we?" the officer chuckled.

"Real funny, Davis," said Charlie. "You're a regular fuckin' comedian."

"And you're a fuckin' junkie! Now go sit your ass in that chair, junkie, right over there next to that bucket."

"Did they get the dope?' I asked Rooster again through the hole in the wall.

"I'm gettin' to it," said Rooster, "but first, let me tell you what happened to Charlie's old lady."

"You mean Janice?"

"Yeah, Janice, Charlie's wife."

A few minutes after Officer Beaumont took Charlie to the dressing room, a female guard told Janice, "Ma'am, please come with me?"

"I'm waitin' for my husband to come back," said Janice.

"Ma'am, I've been told to tell you that your visit's been terminated."

"Terminated!" said Janice. "Why?"

"Ma'am, just please come with me and we'll explain it all to you."

Janice was escorted to the warden's office. There, an attempt was made to interrogate her, but she refused to answer any questions. She was then escorted to the entrance.

Stunned, Janice stood at the base of the tall gun tower, again waiting for the guard to notice her and open the first gate. Again, she looked up, but this time, instead of being blinded by the early-morning sun, she saw dark-gray clouds, black at their base, gathering overhead like giant monsters waiting to pounce. A fierce wind, bringing with it a chill, noisily

shook the razor wire atop the fences. Janice hugged herself, stared down at the sidewalk. Finally, the gate buzzed open and she walked through, once more finding herself locked in a no-man's land between fences.

When the second gate opened, Janice, eager to get as far away from the prison as quickly as possible, hurried through the reception center, then weaved her way through the now-crowded parking lot to find her old Chevrolet. After unlocking the door, she slid behind the wheel, sighed with relief, and turned the key in the ignition. All she heard was a faint click, click, click - then silence. "Damn!" Janice forced herself to breathe deeply, counted to ten, then tried again. This time she heard nothing, not even a faint click, only the sound of the wind buffeting the car. The fragile hold Janice held on her world slipped away. "I knew this was gonna happen!" she screamed into the windshield, then beat the steering wheel with her fists. "I knew it! I told Charlie! I knew it!"

Large raindrops pelted the windshield. Tears rolled down her cheeks. Janice cried, her body wracked with painful convulsions. Then she found an inner strength she didn't know she had. Janice stopped sobbing. She wiped away her tears, then sat quietly for several minutes, staring straight ahead, mesmerized by the patterns of the raindrops zigzagging crazily down the windshield. Then she took a deep breath and sighed, her decision made—

a decision based on not what had just happened, but on an accumulation of disappointments over the past three years. Suddenly Janice felt as light as a feather, as if a heavy burden had been lifted. She turned, reached over the top of the front seat, picked up a baby blanket lying on the back seat, and covered her head. Opening the door, she got out and walked around to the front of the car. Janice lifted the hood and stood there in the pounding rain, staring at the engine and its numerous hoses and wires, remembering what Charlie had said about the solenoid, then realizing that she had no idea what a solenoid looked like or where to find it. Then she heard a voice behind her and turned.

"Excuse me, ma'am," said a man wearing a blue slicker and baseball cap. "Need some help?"

"My car won't start."

"Well, let me take a look at it," said the man, who appeared to be in his early forties.

"Thank you," Janice stepped to the side.

The Good Samaritan pulled on the battery cables. "They're good and tight," he said. "What's it doin'?"

"That's just it, it ain't doin' nothin'. It used to click a few times when I turned the key, but now it don't even do that."

"Clickin'? That sounds like it could be a faulty solenoid."

"That's what my husband said."

"Well, he's probably right. Why don't you get inside out of the rain while I go get a screwdriver outta my truck." Janice climbed inside her car to wait.

When the man returned a few minutes later, he told Janice, "Just turn the key on, but don't try to start it." Under the hood, the man used the screwdriver to bridge the positive poles on the battery and solenoid. The engine started. He closed the hood and walked to the driver's window.

"Oh, thank you, you're a life saver," said Janice. "I don't know what I would have done if you hadn't helped me. Thank you so much."

"My pleasure, ma'am. We all need a little help time to time. Now listen, don't turn the car off 'til you get where you're goin'. Okay."

"I won't. I live in Heflin, about sixty miles from here."

"Heflin," said the man. "I live in Anniston. That's not too far from Heflin. Tell you what. How 'bout I follow you in my truck, just in case it cuts out on you."

"I don't wanna put you out," said Janice. "You've already helped me so much."

"No problem. Like I said, I'm headed that way anyway. My name's Ralph, by the way."

"Janice."

Ralph followed Janice all the way to her door. There, Janice said, "It' still rainin' pretty hard, you wanna come in. I can make you a cup of coffee. It's the least I can do."

"Yeah, sure. I could use a cup. It's been a long night," said Ralph, following Janice inside. There, he removed his slicker, revealing the guard uniform he wore.

Janice was unnerved for a moment but quickly composed herself. "You work at the prison?" she asked.

"Yeah," said Ralph. "I been there about five years now. I usually work nights and get off at seven, but we were short handed this morning, so because of visitation I had to work the front tower."

"I see."

"I work at nights so I can be at home in the afternoon when my girls get outta school," said Ralph. "You see, my wife passed away three years ago."

"Oh, I'm so sorry to hear that."

"She died of breast cancer," said Ralph.

"That's terrible," said Janice. "Musta been hard on you and the kids. How many children you got?"

"Two. Two girls, age eight and ten," said Ralph. "And you. You got kids?"

"Three. Two girls and a boy. Lucy's four and Danielle's eight. My boy, Eddie, he's almost ten. They're at my mother's right now. She keeps 'em for me when I go to work or to Donaldson."

"And your husband?"

"He's in Donaldson. That's who I was visitin' this morning'."

"Oh," said Ralph. "Sorry to hear that. How long's your husband in for?"

"He's got life without parole."

"That's tough," said Ralph.

Chapter Seven
The Plan

"Man, I bet Charlie pitched a fit when he found out that a guard helped Janice get her car started, then invited him inside the house, even served him coffee," I said.

"You don't even know. Gets worse than that," said Rooster.

"Oh yeah."

"I'll tell you about it, but first let me tell you what happened to Charlie in the cell in the infirmary."

"What happened?"

"As soon as me and Hoghead heard they had Charlie locked in a cell in the infirmary, I knew what time it was," said Rooster. "I knew they was gonna' keep him there 'til he shit in that bucket, 'cause the same thing happened to this dude I knew a couple years ago. Kept him in the infirmary for about two days, and he finally caved . . . shit in the bucket."

"And they got the drugs?"

"Yeah, they got 'em. Charged him in court, too. He got an extra five years to go along with the sentence he was already doin'."

"Is that what happened to Charlie?" I asked.

"Hell no!" shouted Rooster. "Weren't no way I was gonna let 'em get that package. I knew I had to figure out somethin' to help Charlie, had to come up with a plan. Then when me and Hoghead went down to the infirmary holdin' cell to talk to Charlie, this idea hit me outta the blue. When I told Hoghead about it, he called me crazy; told me he didn't think it would work, and the truth is, I wasn't too sure myself."

"After you shit in this here bucket," Officer Davis told Charlie, "then the captain might let you outta here—that is, if we don't find no drugs. 'Til then I don't wanna hear no more whinin' outta ya."

"Seems to me, you're the one doin' all the whinin'. I ain't said a word since ya'll kidnapped me," said Charlie.

"Well, you keep it like that and we'll get on just fine," said Officer Davis, smirking. He leaned back in his chair and spit tobacco juice into an empty plastic bottle.

Just look at that stupid bastard, thought Charlie. Happy as a pig rollin' around in shit. And about as smart. I'd like to kick that fuckin' chair out from under him—stomp him in the face, then we'd see who's whinin'."

Officer Davis worked a twelve-hour shift, then was relieved by another guard at six that evening. His relief was a young man who had been working at Donaldson only a few months. The rookie, afraid he may lose his job should he fall asleep during his shift, sat wide-eyed all night, saying very little and watching Charlie like a sentry on duty.

Charlie slept fitfully, the handcuffs biting into his wrists, the duct tape on his ankles too tight, and his stomach cramping. Around midnight, tucked into a fetal position, he thought, Damn, my stomach killin' me. Don't know how long I can hold out, and this is just the first night. And that damn rookie guard. Everytime I look up he's staring at me. That kid ain't blinked once since he came on duty, and he acts like he's afraid to say a word. Man, I need to shit. My stomach's killin' me, but if I do, no doubt that package is comin' out too. Can't shit around it. Despite the discomfort, Charlie smiled at the thought. Now that'd be a trick for sure.

At six the next morning, Officer Davis was back at his post. "Well, good mornin', Sunshine," he told Charlie. "Hope you had a good night. I sure did. My wife fed me a pot roast and homemade mashed potatoes and gravy, then I sat back in my recliner, drank a few beers, watched some football, nailed the old lady, then slept like a baby."

"Fuck you, Davis. Matter of fact, I had a good night, too, and the best part was not havin' to look at your ignorant ass," lied Charlie.

"Yeah, well I'm here now, so deal with it." Officer Davis looked at the food tray on the floor next to the prisoner. "Charlie, you didn't eat your breakfast."

"Ain't hungry," said Charlie.

"Oh, you're gonna get hungry sooner or later. Yes sir, then you'll eat. And guess what's gonna happen then?"

"Shut the fuck up, Davis!" shouted Charlie.

"Damn, Charlie. We're getting' a little touchy, ain't we."

"You know how it is in here," said Rooster through the hole in the wall. "News travels fast." An hour after they put Charlie in that holdin' cell in the infirmary, me and Hoghead heard about it and started makin' plans to get down there and take a look at the situation."

"What're we gonna do now?" Hoghead asked Rooster.

"Well, somehow we need to get down to the infirmary and talk to Charlie. It's plain they didn't get the package off him, else he'd be in the doghouse, not in that lockup cell in the infirmary."

"That makes sense," said Hoghead.

"And that means they're holdin' him 'til he shits out the package. And also that means they got a guard in there watchin' 'im."

"So what we gonna do?"

"Who do we know goes down to the infirmary a lot. . .somebody they don't pay no attention to?" asked Rooster.

"You mean somebody kinda invisible."

"Exactly. Somebody that can move around with no questions asked," said Rooster.

"Hey, how about Old Man Jack, "said Hoghead. "He goes down there four or five times a day. . . practically lives down there."

"I forgot about him," said Rooster. "He's perfect. "All we gotta do is get him to go down there, act crazy like he always does, then come back and let us know what the situation with Charlie is. Think he'll do it?"

"Man, for a couple of cigarettes and a cup of coffee he'll do anything," said Hoghead.

"Go talk to him," said Rooster. "Tell him you'll pay him to go down to the infirmary and check on Charlie for us."

"Yeah, I can do that," said Hoghead. "I get on good with Jack. Most people don't like him, 'cause he's so hard to get along with, but me and him's alright. I actually knew him on the streets. Knew his old man too."

"Good. Go talk to 'im."

Hoghead talked to old man Jack and offered him five cigarettes and two spoons of coffee to go down to the infirmary and find out any information he could regarding Charlie. A couple hours later, Hoghead learned from Jack that Charlie was indeed sitting in the lockdown cell in the infirmary and that he had a guard there with him. More importantly, he learned that the only time that Charlie was left alone was when the guard took a bathroom break. Hoghead asked Jack to go back to the infirmary, hang out there until the guard took another break, then rush back and let him know. Jack complained, but was persuaded by the promise of more cigarettes and coffee.

A few hours later when Officer Davis took a bathroom break, he handcuffed Charlie to an overhead water pipe near the door and left. Jack rushed down the hall (as quickly as possible walking with a cane) and told Rooster and Hoghead. They hurried down the hall to the infirmary holding cell.

Standing behind a locked grille gate, fifteen feet from Charlie, Rooster yelled, "I see they got you hung up like a deer 'bout to be butchered!"

Charlie raised his head and saw Rooster and Hoghead. "It's about time ya'll showed up!"

"Had to wait 'til that guard took a break," said Rooster. "I aint' gonna ask if you got the package, else you wouldn't be hung up like that."

"Damn straight I got it!" yelled Charlie. "And if I wasn't cuffed to this pipe, I could throw it to you before that fucker Davis gets back. I'm gonna tell you, I don't know how much longer I can hold out though, my stomach's crampin' real bad."

"Did you see the captain?" asked Rooster.

"Yeah, I saw his sorry ass yesterday."

"What'd he say?"

"Told me he wouldn't let me out 'til I shit in that bucket you see sittin' over there. And that if he found drugs in it he was gonna put another case on me, plus stop Janice from visitin' me. Hell, he even threatened to charge Janice. . .put her in jail too."

"Can't let that happen," said Rooster.

"I don't know, Rooster," said Charlie. " Maybe I should just give 'em the package. Really, it don't look like I got much choice left. I don't care if they put another charge on me—I got so much time now, a few more years ain't gonna make no difference."

"Well, if you give 'em the package, it'll make a difference to to me and Hoghead, and your old lady. I'd hate to see 'em win, know what I mean."

"Yeah, I know, but."

"Look, just hang in there a little while longer and let me think about it. I promise I'll figure somethin' out. Can you do that?"

"Yeah, I can hang, but don't take too long thinkin', else I'm gonna shit all over myself, and when I do this package is comin' out with it."

"I hear ya'. Now, let me see if I got this right. All you really need is a turd with no dope in it, right?"

"Yeah, but I told you, if I shit in that bucket, this package is comin' out too."

"I know. I know. I'll figure out somethin'. Just hold on 'til Davis takes another break. By then, I'll come up with a plan, I promise. Can you do that?"

"Guess I'll have to," said Charlie.

"Good man," said Rooster. "Just hang in there a little longer. I'll be back."

"Yeah, don't even fart 'til we get back!" laughed Hoghead.

"Fuck you, Hoghead, you big-headed mutherfucker! It ain't funny!"

"Let's go," said Rooster to Hoghead. They turned and walked back down the hall.

Back in the dormitory, Rooster laid back on his bunk, thought about the situation for a while, then came up with an outrageous but simple solution. He explained it to Hoghead. "We're gonna do what!"

Hoghead was incredulous. "Have you lost your fuckin' mind?"

Chapter Eight
The Turd

"Maybe so," said Rooster. "But just think about it. You gotta admit it's a pretty good plan. Makes plenty of sense."

Hoghead walked into the toilet area, stood for a moment and looked around. Seeing a fat man sitting on one of the four exposed toilets, he said, "Hey, big boy, I'm lookin' to buy a good-sized turd. And I got a pack of name brands right here. But it's gotta be big and I gotta have it right now."

"Man, you serious?" asked the fat man.
"Do I look like I'm jokin'?" said Hoghead. "I'm tellin' you, I wanna buy a big turd and I got the smokes on me. Now, how 'bout it?"

"Man, for a pack of smokes, I'll shit you one right now! Just gimme' a few minutes and let me concentrate."

"I'll be back," said Hoghead, walking off.

When Hoghead returned five minutes later, the fat man was standing over the toilet, guarding it. "Well," asked Hoghead. "Had any luck?"

"Damn straight. I gotta beaut for you," said the fat man, pointing at the toilet bowl. "Come see."

Hoghead walked over and looked in the toilet bowl. Floating in the water was a turd the size of a small pepperoni. "That'll do. Here," said Hoghead, handing the fat man a Ziploc bag. "Just fish 'er out and put 'er in this here bag."

"Man, you didn't say I had to touch it!"

"Well, it's your shit! You want the smokes, put it in the bag.

"Damn, I knew there was a catch! Always a catch," said the fat man, reluctantly reaching in the toilet with his bare hand and grabbing the dripping turd.

"Hey, easy!" yelled Hoghead. "Easy. Don't smash it. You smash it, I ain't payin' you!"

"Damn," muttered the fat man, gingerly placing the turd in the plastic bag and handing it to Hoghead.

"Here," said Hoghead, handing the fat man a pack of cigarettes. "Nice doin' business with you."

"A pleasure," said the fat man. "Need any more, let me know. Just give me a heads up."

Hoghead left the toilet area and found Rooster, who was sitting on his bunk drinking a cup of coffee.

"You get it?" asked Rooster.

"Yeah," said Hoghead, holding up the plastic bag like a kid with his first trophy. "It' still warm. Here. Feel it." He extended the bag toward Rooster.

"You crazy son-of-a- bitch!" yelled Rooster. "I don't wanna feel it. Just wrap it in a washcloth and put it in my locker box 'til we can get it down the hall."

Chapter Nine
Fire in the Hole

"You tellin' me you and Hoghead bought a turd!" I laughed into the hole in the wall. "Man, I've been in a lot of prisons and I've seen and heard stuff that would make most people's toes curl, but I ain't never heard of nobody buyin' a turd before."

"Chow Call! Trays on the tier!" shouted a guard, interrupting us.

"Gotta hang up," said Rooster through the hole. "Get ready for this crap they call food."

"I'm so hungry, I don't give a damn what it is," I said. "Just hope they put plenty on the tray."

"Good luck with that. They hardly feed enough to keep a bird alive. Look, I'll holler at you later," said Rooster, plugging the hole.

After a supper of cold greens, a soybean patty, pinto beans, cornbread, and melted Jello, I lay down.

The next day Rooster said through the hole in the wall, "Know what today is?"

"Sure, it's Sunday," I said.

"True that," said Rooster, "but it's the fourth Sunday of the month. Know what that means?"

"What?"

"Means it's chicken Sunday," said Rooster.

"Chicken Sunday?"

"Yeah, chicken Sunday. Every fourth Sunday we get fried chicken and all the fixin's, even apple cobbler."

"You gotta be kiddin'."

"I'm serious," said Rooster. "You'll see."

In the doghouse, the menu was monotonous; the food bland and always cold. But every fourth Sunday was a day of respite. All the prisoners at Donaldson, including those in the doghouse, were served fried chicken, a heaping of mashed potatoes and gravy, English peas and carrots, a dinner roll, and a generous portion of apple cobbler.

The food cart arrived about two-thirty to find most of the doghouse prisoners eagerly waiting near their tray hole. When the cart stopped in front of my cell and the kitchen worker, accompanied by a guard, pushed a tray through the hole, I immediately noticed that one of the food slots on the plastic tray was empty. On the tray was a chicken thigh, mashed potatoes, a roll, peas and carrots, but no apple cobbler. I beat on the wall. "Yeah," said Rooster.

"I thought you said we get apple cobbler."

"We do," said Rooster.

"Well, I didn't get none on my tray."

"No shit. You was suppose to," said Rooster. "Wait a minute, my tray's comin' through the hole now." Then I heard Rooster yell at the kitchen worker. "Hey man, me and cell four didn't get no apple cobbler!" The kitchen worker and guard ignored Rooster and continued on down the line passing out trays.

I heard another prisoner just a few cells down yell, "Where's the fuckin' pie!" And then another: "Hey man, this slot's empty! We always get apple cobbler! Where's the fuckin' apple cobbler!"

Then someone down the line started banging on his stainless steel sink with the heel of his brogan. Another followed suit. Several raked the steel bars with their cups.

The kitchen worker passing out the trays yelled, "Look, we're outta apple cobbler, so everybody just shut the fuck up!"

"Who the fuck you talkin' to like that!" yelled a prisoner in a cell on the top tier. "What! You the police now! You wouldn't talk like that I could get my hands on 'ya!"

Someone else yelled: "I betcha that bastard handin' out the trays got some apple cobbler!"

"Damn straight!" yelled an irate prisoner. He struck a match and set fire to a roll of toilet paper, then threw it out the tray slot like a Molotov cocktail. "Let's burn this fucker down!" he yelled. Other prisoners followed suit, throwing flaming sheets, towels, blankets, and even pants and shirts out the tray hole.

"Here, you eat this shit!" shouted a prisoner, throwing his entire tray back out the tray slot. More trays followed, splattering mashed potatoes and peas and carrots in the hall and against the far wall.

Dodging flaming missiles and trays, the guard and the kitchen worker, abandoned the food cart and ran for the door at the end of the hall.

Smoke quickly filled the cellblock, making it impossible to breathe or see. I plugged my sink and toilet with rags, then flushed and reflushed the toilet until I had an inch of water on the floor of my cell. I lay down flat on my back on the floor, covered my face with a wet towel, and waited.

Before long, several guards entered the doghouse wearing protective masks and carrying a long, canvas, fireman's hose. Stretching it the length of the hall, they used the hose's water pressure not only to extinguish the dozens of small fires in the cells and the hall but to wash mounds of smoking debris out the back door.

But the guards manning the hose couldn't keep up, because as soon as one fire was extinguished, another popped up as prisoners continued to throw flaming objects at the guards. The tactical unit was summoned. When they arrived they dragged the arsonists from their cells one at a time, handcuffed them, beat them, then hauled them out the door at the end of the hall and locked them in the cages outside.

After all the fires were extinguished, two trustees, supervised by a guard, used brooms and squeezes to push the remaining debris and water out the open door. Then they set up large floor fans to blow away the lingering smoke. When it was all over, the mood in the doghouse was somber. It was as eerily quiet as a city street after a F-5 tornado had passed.

Two hours later, the food cart returned, quietly moving from cell to cell passing out fresh food trays loaded with chicken, mashed potatoes, peas and carrots, a dinner roll, and a generous portion of apple cobbler.

After eating, I beat on the wall and unplugged the hole. "Rooster!" I yelled. "You alright over there?"

"Hell, yeah," coughed Rooster. "I'm good. Just tryin' to get some of this black shit outta my nose and throat. How about you?"

"Yeah, I'm good too. The smoke and soot didn't get me too bad 'cause I flooded my cell, covered my face with a wet towel and laid down on the floor."

"I shoulda done that. Didn't think of it."

"I learned that after my first fire in lockup years ago," I said. "When I was in Plaquemines Parish prison in south Louisiana, this dude in the cell next to me set his mattress on fire. The cells down there was old style, you know, built outta steel with those big rivets they used back then, and the smoke got so thick you couldn't even see the wall. And they didn't have a sprinkler system, so those steel walls got as hot as the inside of a coffee pot on a hot stove. That's when I learned that the best thing to do was to get wet and get low."

"What happened to the dude set his mattress on fire?" asked Rooster.

"Died from breathin' all that smoke before they could get to him."

"Man, I can understand settin' somethin' in the cell on fire and throwin' it out in the hallway," said Rooster, "but what kinda' fool's gonna set his mattress on fire when he knows he can't get his mattress through the tray hole, and sure as hell can't get outta the cell?"

"A fool ain't thinkin', you ask me," I said.

"Well, that apple cobbler was good, but it wouldn't worth all that," mused Rooster.

"You know well as I do, settin' the cellblock on fire didn't have much to do with not getting' apple cobbler," I said. "It was the principle of the thing. These dudes in the doghouse felt they was being chumped off, disrespected—figured if they let 'em get away with takin' one thing from 'em, the next thing you know they'll be sendin' trays over here with no chicken on 'em. You lose anything?"

"I didn't set nothin' on fire - well, except a roll of toilet paper, and I had a couple extra rolls anyway, but no way was I gonna burn up all my shit like some of these idiots. I need my towel and blanket and clothes. Winter's comin' and sometimes it gets cold up in here," said Rooster.

"Well, it's over now," I said, "and since we're already up here at the hole, you can finish tellin' me how this masterplan you came up with worked out."

Chapter Ten
What Goes in Gotta Come Out

"Alright," said Rooster. "Well, it wasn't too long, maybe an hour and a half, 'til Old Man Jack showed up. Me and Hoghead was sittin' on the bed when Jack walks up and says: 'That guard down there at the infirmary just took himself a break.' So I put on my jacket, reached into my locker box, got the Ziploc bag with the turd in it, put the bag in the sleeve of my coat, and me and Hoghead headed down the hall to the infirmary holdin' cell. Again, we found Charlie handcuffed to the overhead water pipe."

At the grille gate, Rooster shouted, "Charlie!"

"'What's up?' shouted back Charlie. "Look, said Rooster, holdin' up the plastic bag. I gotcha a turd."

"You got what!"

"A turd," said Rooster. "I gotcha a turd to put in that bucket."

"Are you outta your fuckin' mind!" yelled Charlie.

"Probably," said Rooster. "But look Charlie, we ain't got much time, so listen. Hoghead's gonna throw this turd to ya', and when you get it put it in the bucket."

"How am I supposed to do that! My hands is cuffed to this water pipe."

"Damn, Charlie! I gotta do all your thinkin' for 'ya! Use your feet! And when you get it, hide it 'til you can get it in that bucket without Davis seein' ya. Got me?"

"Alright! Alright! I'll try. Go ahead and throw it to me."

Hoghead, once again the small boy on the school yard pitching pennies to the line, reached through the steel bars, took careful aim and tossed the Ziploc bag underhanded. The bag hit the floor two feet from the holding cell door and slid.

"Damn!" shouted Charlie. "I hate to admit it, but that was a helluva throw! I can see the edge of the bag sticking under the door."

"I told you I ain't nothin' to play with!" shouted back Hoghead.

"Hoghead, you're a throwin' fool!" said Rooster, slapping Hoghead on the back. He then said to Charlie. "Think you can get it from there?"

"Think so," said Charlie.

"Don't think so, just do it," said Rooster. "We ain't got time for thinkin'."

Rooster and Hoghead watched as Charlie, like a prisoner hanging from a medieval torture rack, braced himself with one leg, then stretched out the other. He pressed the toe of his shoe on the edge of the plastic bag and slowly dragged it under the door. Then, as adept as a soccer player, Charlie maneuvered the plastic bag behind a broom leaning against the wall. He yelled to Rooster and Hoghead, "I got it! I got that motherfucker!"

"Alright!" shouted Rooster. "It's all up to you now!"

"Yeah, Charlie!" shouted Hoghead. "Don't fuck this up like you usually do!"

"I got this, Bighead! Don't sweat it!"

Rooster and Hoghead left just ahead of Officer Davis, who released Charlie from the water pipe and handcuffed his hands in front.

A few minutes later, Charlie asked Officer Davis, "Mind if I sweep up? I'm tired of just sittin'."

"Well now Charlie, that's damn nice of you. Go ahead and sweep if you want. You mind if I just sit here and watch?"

Charlie glared at the guard, then walked over, grabbed the broom, and - blocking Officer Davis' view with his body - furtively swept the plastic bag behind the five-gallon bucket. He then carefully swept the entire cell.

While Charlie swept, Officer Davis reached in his back pocket and retrieved a foil pouch of chewing tobacco. He put a plug the size of a ping pong ball in his mouth, chewed a few times, then pushed it around with his tongue, slowly sucking the juice from it. Officer Davis leaned over and spat in a plastic Gatorade bottle. Looking at the inmate, he said, "Charlie, this is your second day, and let's face it, sooner or later you're gonna' have to shit. That's just nature."

"What you know about nature?" asked Charlie, continuing to sweep.

"I know what goes in gotta come out. I know that." Officer Davis smirked, as if he had just come up with a truly clever and original statement.

"I think it's: 'What goes up gotta come down.'"

"Same thing," said Officer Davis.

"You know what, Davis. Now that you mention it, I do feel a shit comin' on."

"You serious." Officer Davis looked both interested and hopeful. He rolled the plug to his other cheek.

"Yep, I think so. Take these cuffs off me so I can wipe my ass. Gimme a roll of toilet paper and I'll give it a try."

"Dammit, Charlie! Now that's what I'm talkin' about. Give us a good shit, then we can both get outta here."

Charlie walked to Officer Davis and held out his hands. The guard removed his handcuffs, then handed him a roll of toilet paper. Charlie went to the bucket, pulled down his pants and sat on it with his back against the wall. Leaning forward, his forearms on his upper thighs, he pretended to strain while secretly watching Officer Davis, who was now cleaning his fingernails with a penknife. Charlie leaned forward a little more and placed the roll of toilet paper on the floor. He slowly reached behind the bucket, and just as he attempted to grab the Ziploc bag, Officer Davis looked up. Charlie froze, grunted, and pretended to strain. The guard returned to his nails. Again Charlie slowly reached behind, and this time he was able to grab the Ziploc bag with the tips of his fingers. Lifting his butt, he emptied the baggie into the bucket. The turd hit with a plop. Officer Davis looked up again. Again Charlie pretended to strain. The guard spit into his plastic bottle, then returned to his nails. Charlie stuffed the plastic bag into the center of the roll of tissue, wiped, then set the roll of toilet paper on the floor. He stood and pulled up his pants, looked over at Officer Davis and said, "Hey Davis, I got somethin' for ya'." Charlie picked up the roll of toilet tissue and stepped away from the bucket.

"Well, it's about time. Let's have a look."

Officer Davis walked over and looked in the bucket. "Damn, Charlie, that's all."

"What the fuck you want? . . . a whole bucketful! Just look at the size of that turd. Man, you know how hard I had to work to get that out!"

"Well, with all that gruntin' you was doin', I expected to see a lot more than that." Officer Davis stretched rubber gloves over his freshly-manicured hands, reached into the bucket, broke the turd apart, and carefully searched it.

While the guard was occupied, Charlie removed the Ziploc bag from the center of the toilet paper roll and put it in his back pocket.

Officer Davis turned to the inmate. "Looks clean to me. Huh." He frowned at Charlie.

"See, I told ya!" shouted Charlie. "I told you and the captain both I ain't got no drugs! I oughta sue both of ya'!"

"Hey, if that floats your boat, go ahead. I been sued before."

"When ya gonna let me outta' here, Davis?"

"That's up to the captain."

Chapter Eleven
Man, That's Some Good Shit

An hour later Charlie was released from the infirmary holding cell. Bent over, his stomach cramping, he hurried down the hall, every step threatening to jar loose the drug package. He rushed through the dormitory door and straight to the toilet. Quickly dropping his pants, he sat down, his insides erupting like a volcano. "Ahhh," he sighed.

Hoghead and Rooster saw Charlie rush into the dormitory and followed him to the restroom. "Thought you might need this," said Rooster, tossing Charlie a roll of toilet paper.

"Might need two rolls," said Charlie. "Damn, that felt good." Charlie wiped, pulled up his pants, and looked in the toilet. "Let's see what we got." He reached inside and grabbed the dripping drug package. "Here, make yourself useful, Fathead," he told Hoghead, handing him the drug package. "Rinse this off."

"Fuck!" said Hoghead, walking over to the sink.

Later, while Hoghead stood by the door watching for an unexpected arrival of a guard, Rooster and Charlie sat on Rooster's bed, the drug package on a sheet of newspaper. When Rooster slit it open with a razor blade, the compressed pot, free of its binding, blossomed like a flower seen through time-lapse photography, covering the newspaper in marijuana and pills.

Rooster and Charlie separated the ounce of marijuana into twelve separate piles (each pile representing a matchbox), then wrapped each in cellophane saved from cigarette packs. "Let's sell ten, then smoke the other two," Rooster said to Charlie.

"The fuck with that," said Charlie. "We'll sell six and smoke six. I ain't gotta' send Janice but three-hundred."

"You sure?"

"Yeah."

"Wanna sell the pills too?" asked Rooster.

"Hell no," said Charlie. "Me, you and Hoghead's gonna eat those. That's our reward for all the shit we had to go through."

Later, sitting on the bunk, Hoghead exhaled a cloud of blue smoke, sighed contentedly, and said, "Man, that's some good shit!" He took another big hit, holding the smoke in his lungs until it burned. Slowly exhaling, a smile spreading across his broad face, he repeated, "Man, that's some good shit!" He passed the joint to Rooster.

Rooster took an equally big hit and said, "It's good, alright, but smells like shit!" They all laughed. Rooster passed the joint to Charlie.

Charlie took a hit, exhaled, and said, "Ought to . . . been in my ass for two days!" They all laughed uncontrollably.

In less than a week, Rooster, Hoghead and Charlie smoked nine matchboxes and sold only three. Hoghead and Charlie ate the pills like breath mints.

"Looks like everything worked out pretty good," I told Rooster through the hole in the wall. "But that still don't tell me how you ended up in the doghouse."

"I know. I know," said Rooster. "It wasn't what happened before we scored, but what happened after that landed me and Charlie in the doghouse."

"What about Hoghead? He go to the doghouse, too?"

"Nah. Hoghead didn't go to the doghouse - well not with me and Charlie. He went, but for only thirty days," said Rooster. "You see, when him and Charlie started eatin' all them pills, Hoghead went buck-wild. He bought himself a gallon of homemade wine some dude made outta raisins, took about five of them Valium, and got into a fight with some dude in the TV room. Anyhow, they put him in the doghouse for thirty days. But all that happened before me and Charlie got locked up."

Only after Charlie had taken the last pill and smoked the last joint did he sober up enough to think to call Janice. When he called, he got a recording: "Sorry, your call was not accepted. Please try again." Charlie called over and over, but got the same recording every time. "Damn!" he shouted, slamming the phone into the receiver. Wonder what the problem is? he asked himself.

Two days later, Charlie received a short letter from Janice telling him not to call or write anymore, and that she was filing for divorce. She wrote that she had met someone, a "decent man."

Charlie complained to Hoghead and Rooster: "I can't believe that ungrateful bitch! Treating me like that after all I done for her and them stinkin' brats! Took 'em in, treated 'em like they was my own too!"

A few days later, Charlie asked Rooster, "What we gonna do now?"

"I been thinkin' about it," said Rooster, "and what we need is to get our money together, then we need to figure out how to score again. You know, all we got is a hundred fifty dollars."

"Remember, Waco and Patch still owe us a hundred from time before last. Want me to ask Waco for it when I see 'im tomorrow morning?" said Charlie.

"Yeah, do that, and I'll try to figure out how we can get somebody to score for us."

The next day around noon, Rooster asked Charlie, "Waco pay you that hundred?"

"Fuck no!" said Charlie. "I asked 'im for it this mornin' when I saw 'im at the laundry, and he told me he'd pay me when he got it. But shit, that's the same thing he told me a couple weeks ago. Acted like he was pissed 'cause I asked 'im for it."

"Man, I don't give a fuck he's pissed or not!" shouted Rooster. "I'm pissed, too! Pissed 'cause this son of a bitch smoked our dope and now he don't wanna pay for it! Tell you what, I'll ask 'im myself."

That evening after supper, Rooster and Charlie waited in the hall for Waco and his sidekick, Patch, a one-eyed man in his late forties.

Waco was a big man, almost as large as Hoghead. He was a bully with a surly disposition, and most in Donaldson avoided him. Rooster looked up at Waco and said politely, "Look, Waco, me and Charlie really need that hundred you owe us, or else I wouldn't be buggin' you about it."

"I told your partner here this mornin' that I'll pay you when I get it. Can't do no more than that."

"That's what he told me, and I wouldn't keep askin', except we need that money to make another score. So when you think you'll have it?"

"When!" shouted Waco. "When I get it, that's when!"

"But look, we gotta'. . ."

"You look, asshole . . . and listen!", interrupted Waco. "You're startin' to get on my nerves, hear me. So you best quit buggin' me about a measly hundred dollars!" When Waco turned to leave, Rooster grabbed the big man's arm. Waco turned and grabbed Rooster by the shirt. He lifted him to his toes and threw him against the wall, holding him there. "You know what, little man, you done fucked up and made me lose my temper," said Waco. "I've changed my mind. You can just chalk that hundred up; I ain't payin' you nothin'. Now, how you like that? No, I'll tell you what, you want that money so bad, you just get it like the Red Cross!" Waco released Rooster, then shoved him. The smaller man stumbled, then regained his footing.

"Okay, big man," said Rooster, straightening his clothes. "Know it when you see it."

"You threatin' me?" said Waco. Rooster didn't answer. Instead, he just stared Waco in the eyes. Finally, Waco turned and said to Patch, "Let's go. These chumps ain't gonna do nothin'." They left Charlie and Rooster standing in the hall.

Rooster was so angry that he didn't say a word until he and Charlie were back in the dormitory and sitting on his bed. Then he said to Charlie, "I'm gonna' get that big bastard. Get it like the Red Cross! I can't believe he told me to get it like the Red Cross! Okay, he wants me to get it in blood, that's exactly how we're gonna get it. . . in blood! That bastard ain't gonna know what hit 'im!"

"I don't know who the fuck he thinks he is," said Charlie. "It's a good thing Hoghead wasn't there. He would've jumped his big ass right there in the hall."

"We oughta strap down right now and go over to Waco's dorm, stick him and that one-eyed bastard, Patch," said Charlie. Who the fuck does he think he is. . . Superman?"

"Oh, he ain't no Superman, you can believe that. He bleeds just like everybody else, but listen Charlie, we gotta be smart about this." Rooster paused. "We gotta be patient and use the element of surprise. We gotta catch 'em when they ain't expectin' it."

Chapter Twelve
Get It Like the Red Cross

Rooster's pride was hurt, but more important, his status was in jeopardy. He knew that he couldn't allow anyone to disrespect him the way Waco had, not if he wanted to continue to do business at Donaldson, so he decided to make an example of Waco and his partner, Patch.

That night, Rooster and Charlie stayed up late, smoking cigarettes, drinking coffee, and planning. After only a couple hours sleep, they were up early the next morning.

Charlie walked down the hall to Patch's dormitory. Under his shirt he carried a homemade ice pick with a six-inch blade. He found Patch in bed asleep. Charlie stabbed Patch in his good eye, blinding him. Patch screamed and sat up in bed, holding his face with both hands, blood dripping from his outstretched fingers, soaking his bed sheet. Charlie put the ice pick in his waistband, covered it with his shirt, then calmly walked out of the dorm, passing an unsuspecting guard standing in the hall.

At almost the same time Rooster stood outside the door to Waco's dormitory waiting for him to exit. In his hands, he held an aluminum softball bat that he had stolen out of the recreation shack. When Waco stepped through the door, Rooster slammed him in the knees with the bat, toppling the big man

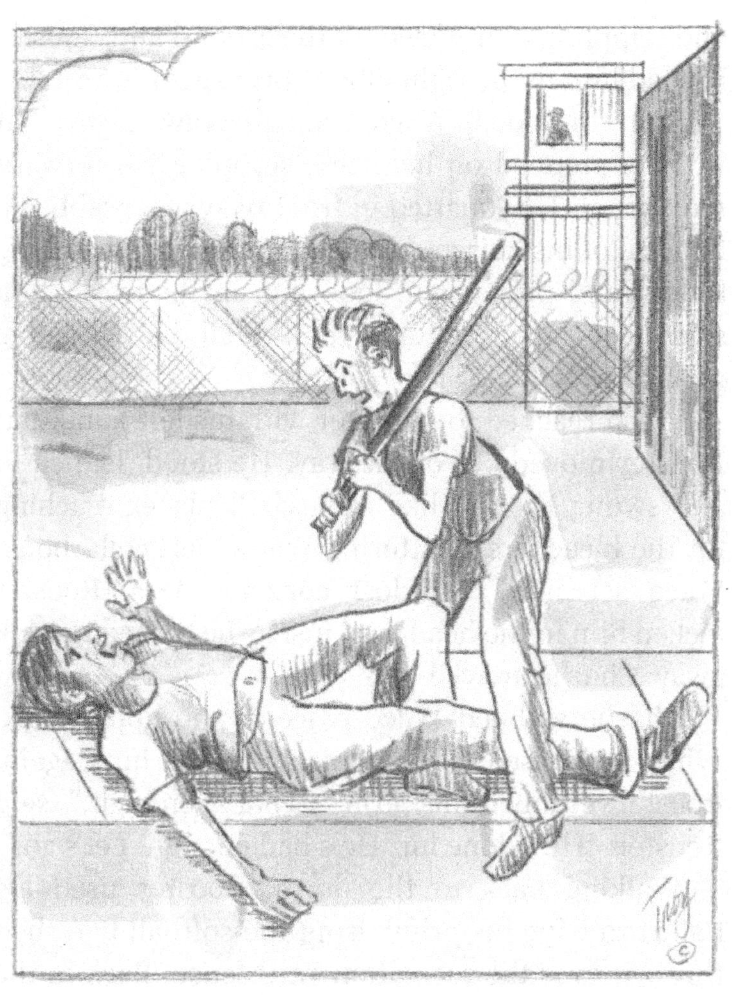

and crippling him. Waco hit the ground and Rooster bashed him in the right elbow, breaking his arm.

Still conscious, Waco tried to crawl away, but Rooster stepped on his neck, stopping his forward movement. He squatted in front of Waco, grabbed a handful of his hair and jerked his head back, forcing the injured prisoner to look him in the eyes. "You said, 'Get it like the Red Cross!' Well, here it is, big man. How you like it!"

Waco reached for Rooster with his left hand, but Rooster moved out of the way. He stood, leaned in and swung the bat like a baseball player reaching for the bleachers, shattering Waco's left collarbone. Waco screamed and lost consciousness. Rooster kicked him in the head, and just as he turned to walk away, Charlie arrived.

Charlie stabbed Waco twice in the upper back. When he raised the ice pick to stab him again, Rooster grabbed his arm. "That's enough," said Rooster. "He's done for. He's had enough. Let's go."

Walking back to the dorm, Rooster used his t-shirt to wipe his prints from the softball bat, then threw it over the recreation yard fence. Back in the dormitory, Charlie flushed the ice pick down the toilet, then joined Rooster who was sitting on his bed smoking a cigarette. "You get Patch?" Rooster asked Charlie.

"Yeah, you know it. I got that bastard good . . . stabbed him in his good eye, blinded 'im." Just then, a siren blared over the loudspeakers, chilling the hearts of prisoners and guards alike.

"Well, I guess they found 'em," said Rooster.

"What we gonna' do now?" asked Charlie.

"Nothin' to do," said Rooster. "It's all been done. Now, we just wait."

"I need a cigarette," said Charlie.

"Here," said Rooster, handing Charlie the short on the cigarette he'd been smoking.

They didn't have to wait long. Before Charlie even finished smoking the cigarette, eight guards ran into the dormitory and headed straight for Rooster's bed. And even though they offered no resistance, Rooster and Charlie were slammed to the concrete floor before being handcuffed and taken to the doghouse.

Chapter Thirteen
The Gift of Understanding

"And that's it," said Rooster into the hole in the wall. "That's how me and Charlie ended up in the doghouse."

"Man, that's a helluva story," I said. "I can't believe Charlie stabbed that one-eyed dude in his good eye. That's cold."

"Hey, prison's a cold world and Charlie could be a cruel son-of-a-bitch," said Rooster. "Plus, he was already pissed off 'cause Janice wrote him that Dear John. Guess he took his frustration out on Patch. Who knows?"

"And that's another thing I was gonna ask you about Charlie. You told me a few days ago that he died, but you didn't tell me how he died. Did he die in the doghouse?" I asked.

"No, not exactly. He died in a lockup cell in the infirmary," said Rooster. "You see, Charlie had hepatitis C. He got real sick and they had to take him outta the doghouse and put him in the infirmary. Charlie wouldn't take his medication and so his liver got all messed up. Guess it was all that dope he used to shoot when he was on the streets. You shoulda seen him. He got kinda bloated-like. His legs swelled up, he couldn't use the toilet, his nuts swelled up to the size of grapefruits, he couldn't walk—he couldn't even stand up long enough for us to talk through this hole in the wall. Finally, he got so sick he couldn't even get his tray outta the tray hole. Lost weight, weren't nothin' but skin and bones."

"I told the guard when he made his rounds, but he wouldn't do nothin' Finally when the chaplin came around on Sunday, I told him. He took one look at Charlie and got him moved to a holdin' cell in the infirmary. There, they looked at him, took some tests, then the doctor told Charlie his liver was all fucked up and he only had a few months to live."

"Damn, that's fucked up," I said. "How long did he make it?"

"Well, accordin' to what this dude works in the infirmary told me, not too long."

Every day, an inmate volunteer was allowed inside the holding cell to attend Charlie. Most days Charlie's mind was clear, and on those days he and the volunteer talked for hours. Sometimes the volunteer read to him, but on the days when the pain was so intense that Charlie couldn't concentrate on anything but the pain, the worker just sat quietly with him.

As the disease spread and the pain increased, Charlie was given a liquid narcotic twice daily, and in a slurred voice he always asked for more, even though the powerful medication constipated him and caused him to sit on the toilet for hours. When that happened the inmate volunteer sat in a chair nearby and he and Charlie talked, Charlie often dozing off in the middle of a sentence only to awaken a few minutes later and continue as if there had been no pause in their conversation.

Charlie's appetite decreased and sometimes he vomited blood. Whenever that happened, the inmate volunteer alerted the nurses and they did what they could to comfort him. Then one day, Charlie seemed to make a miraculous recovery. His pain eased and the swelling in his body diminished. Charlie's appetite returned, and he ate all he could get his hands on. His mind cleared. Then Charlie did the unexpected: He asked to see the prison chaplain.

A kind and compassionate man, the chaplain visited Charlie in his cell. He sat beside him and prayed. Afterward, tears in his eyes, Charlie told the chaplain: "You know, Chaplain, I been greedy and selfish all my life."

"Charlie, most of us have been greedy and selfish at one time or another," said the chaplain.

"But you don't understand, Chaplain, I been like that my whole life. Seems I ain't never been able to get enough—not enough food, not enough money, not enough sex, and never enough drugs. Especially drugs. And now those drugs done killed me, and my wife done divorced me. Now I ain't got nobody in the world loves me, all because of the way I done lived my life."

"God loves you," said the chaplain. "God always cares."

"I know that now, Chaplain, and I believe it, but you know what I mean. I ain't got nobody in this world that loves me, and it's because I been so selfish and greedy, only caring about what I wanted." The chaplain sat quietly and let Charlie talk. "I ain't never been satisfied," continued Charlie. "And I been doin' a lot of thinkin' lately, and I'm thinkin' that maybe, just maybe, what I been tryin' to find with all those drugs, was not just another high, but love. Does that make any sense?"

"Sure, it does Charlie," said the chaplin. "Makes plenty of sense. We all want love. The problem is that we don't always pursue love in healthy ways. I believe that you've got to love God first, or maybe Charlie, you just got to let God love you first, then you'll learn to love yourself. I mean genuinely love who you are before you can ever learn to love another person."

"Well, I never could find whatever it was I was lookin' for with the drugs 'cause the highest high always wore off, and then all I was left with was the lowest low. And to tell you the truth, I'm not even sure that I ever really knowed what love is. I mean, what love really is. But now I think I know what it ain't. It ain't all those things I been chasin' all my life."

"I believe that you're on the right track now, Charlie," said the chaplin And I believe that through the grace of God, you've finally been given the gift of understanding. Now, let's pray."

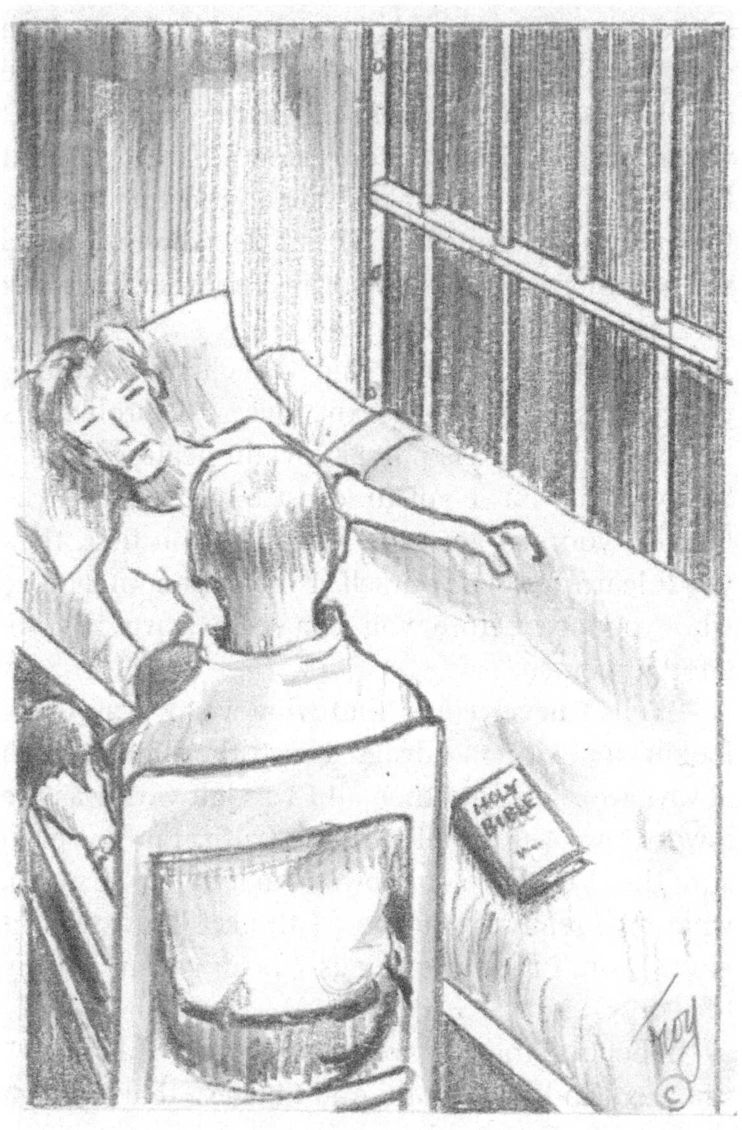
HOLY
BIBLE

That afternoon, the disease that had destroyed Charlie's body ate his will to live too, and Charlie died peacefully in his sleep that night."

"You're tellin me that Charlie got religion in the end?" I said into the hole in the wall.

"I don't know what he got - if he got religion, saw the Light, or whatever, but he got somethin'," said Rooster.

Chapter Fourteen
Jack

A couple days later, when Rooster and I were taken outside for fresh air and exercise, we were put in cages in separate areas. In the cage next to me was a short, gray haired old man. Standing in a far corner of the cage, he had one hand propped on a cane, the other holding onto the fence. He stared out at the thick woods a couple hundred yards distant.

Like a dog released into unfamiliar territory I circled the perimeter of the cage. When I came near the old man, I said, "What's up, old timer?"

The old man didn't acknowledge me; instead he continued to hold onto the fence and stare into the woods. I thought, Either he didn't hear me or wants to be left alone. I'll just leave him alone. I continued to circle the cage.

A few minutes later when I came close again, the old man turned and asked, "Got a smoke?"

"I don't smoke," I said.

"Humph," grunted the old man, turning his back on me and continuing to stare into the woods.

Later, through the hole in the wall, I said to Rooster, "You know when I went on walk this mornin', I got put in a cage next to this weird, little old man. He was just standin' in a corner of the cage starin' into the woods, like he was in a trance or somethin'"

"What'd he look like?" asked Rooster.

"Well, he was about five-four, I guess. Had this wild gray hair and used a walking cane," I said. "To tell you the truth, what he looked like to me was . . . you know that cereal they sell, Lucky Charms."

"Yeah."

"Well, on the box they got a little leprechaun in a green hat and suit. That's who he looked like. He was dead ringer for that leprechaun on a box of Lucky Charms."

Rooster laughed. "That's Old Man Jack. Can't be nobody else. Remember I told ya when they had Charlie in the imfimary holdin' cell, we got this old man to post up down at the infirmary to let us know when the guard left?"

"Yeah."

"That's Jack. I heard he was in the doghouse. One of them kitchen workers that brings the trays up here told me. Said Jack hit some dude in the head with that cane of his. Split the dude's head wide open, and they gave him thirty days in the doghouse." Rooster paused, then continued. "I tell you one thing about Jack, he might be a little, old man, but he ain't harmless. He'll take on a gorilla if it fucks with 'im." And then, through the hole in the wall, Rooster told me how Jack ended up in the doghouse.

Jack, an unlit cigarette dangling from his pursed lips, walked up to Hoghead who was leaning against the wall in the TV area smoking a cigarette. "Got a light?" asked Jack.

"Sure, Jack," said Hoghead, offering his lit cigarette. When Jack leaned forward to light his cigarette, a young, muscular prisoner sneaked up behind Jack and jabbed him in the ribs.

Startled, Jack dropped his cane. Wheeling around, he stumbled, then braced himself against the wall. "Dammit, you sumbitch!" yelled Jack. "Don't poke me like that!" On shaky legs, Jack carefully stooped to pick up his cane, but before he could grab it, the young prisoner scooped it up.

"Dammit, you sumbitch!" yelled Jack. "Gimme back my cane!"

"You want it, come get it, you smelly, old bastard!" shouted the young prisoner, gleefully dancing around, waving the cane like a band leader.

Jack stepped closer and the other prisoner held out the cane, but when Jack reached out, the young man snatched it away. "Man, you're way too slow," he laughed. "Here, try again." Again, he held out the cane, and again when Jack reached for it, the prisoner snatched it out of his reach.

Enraged, frustrated, and out of breath, Jack gave up. He walked over to a bench and sat down, looked up at the prisoner and said quietly, "I'm gonna'. . . get you . . you sumbitch. You just wait."

"Jerry," said Hoghead to the young prisoner holding Jack's cane, "you keep messin' with old Jack here, and I'm tellin' you, one of these days he's gonna sneak up on you and bust your brains out."

"Him!" shouted Jerry. "That smelly old bastard's too fuckin' slow to catch me like that!"

"You just keep thinkin' that," said Hoghead, "but I'm here to tell you, ain't always the fastest wins the race."

"Huh," said Jerry. "What the hell's that mean?"

"Maybe you'll figure it out . . . you live long enough. The graveyard's full of young dudes never did."

Jerry threw the cane down and walked off. Hoghead picked it up, walked over and handed it to the old man. "He didn't mean nothin', Jack," said Hoghead. "Just playin'."

"I'm gonna' get that sumbitch," said Jack. "I don't like nobody playin' with me."

A couple of weeks later, while sitting on one of the TV benches watching the evening news, Hoghead heard someone behind him yell, then the sound of a wooden bench scraping the floor. He turned to see Jerry on his knees between two benches. He was holding his bloody head with both hands. Over him stood Jack, his cane raised to strike again. "I told you I'd get you, you sumbitch,!" yelled Jack, panting.

"Damn!" shouted Jerry, holding onto the bench with one hand, while staunching the flow of blood from a deep cut over his right eye with the other. "You old bastard, I'm gonna kill you for this!" Jack cracked him on top of his head. Jerry yelled, covered his head with his hands, and crawled under the bench.

"Someone shouted: "The guards! They're comin'." Jack quickly threw his cane under a bunk, dropped to the floor and rolled onto his back.

The two guards rushed through the door, saw Jack moaning on the floor, and rushed over. The first guard to reach Jack, said, "What's wrong, old timer?"

"My back," moaned Jack. "My back's hurt." He pointed at Jerry, now sitting on the bench pressing his t-shirt to his head. "He jumped me."

The second guard walked over to where Jerry sat. "You jump on that old man?" he asked.

"Hell no!" cried Jerry. "He's the one jumped me! Look at my head! He hit me with that damn cane of his!"

"Now, I seriously doubt that," said the guard. "That old man's twice your age."

"I'm tellin' you," wailed Jerry. "He's lyin'. He's the one hit me! Look at my head!"

"We'll see about that. Now, stand up!" Jerry stood and the guard, ignoring the still-bleeding cut over Jerry's eye, handcuffed him.

Jack and Jerry were both taken to the infirmary. Then, because it was uncertain who had done what to whom, they were both sent to the doghouse for thirty days.

Chapter Fifteen
Population

The night before I was to be released into the general prison population, I unplugged the hole in the wall one last time. "Well, they tell me they're gonna let me out in population tomorrow," I told Rooster.

"Man, wish I was goin' with you."

"Well, you ain't got much longer," I said.

"Less than two months, that's all."

"That ain't nothin' for a stepper," I joked.

"Yeah, you got that right. I can do two months sittin' on the shitter if I have to," said Rooster.

"What do they say? It won't be as long as it has been . . ."

"And it won't be as short as it will be," said Rooster. "Oh, one more thing before you head out. Look up Hoghead. He's livin' in Two Dorm. Tell 'im to send me a couple packs of smokes if he can. Tell 'im to give 'em to that kitchen worker brings the trays to the doghouse. Oh, and I probably don't need to remind you, but I will anyway, here at Donaldson, you are judged by who you hang out with, so watch out who you associate with."

"It's like that in all the prison's I been in," I said, "but I appreciate the reminder. I kinda stay to myself anyway. I'm not what you'd call a social person. I've found it's just a lot easier that way, and if I get into some shit, it's me got me into it not somebody else."

Rooster laughed. "I just thought of somethin' else I wanted to tell you."

"What's that?"

"Just a crazy thought I had last night."

"Alright, go ahead. Tell me."

"Well, we're in the hole, right," said Rooster.

"Yeah."

"And me and you been talkin' through a hole in the wall, right."

"Yeah."

"So, what we got is a hole in the hole! Get it!" laughed Rooster. "We got a hole in the hole!"

"Man, you really need to get outta here," I laughed. "You're finally losin' it. You keep havin' thoughts like that, you're gonna end up in a padded cell with Sidewinder! You ain't been smokin' that shit again, have you?"

"I wish!" shouted Rooster. "I could use me a good joint 'bout now."

The next morning, I was released from the doghouse and sent to live in Donaldson's general population.

Dragging my mattress and carrying my laundry bag, I struggled down the long hall from the doghouse to the control center. There, the guard told me that I had been assigned to bed eighty-two in Two Dorm, the same dormitory that Hoghead lived in.

I found Two Dorm and my bunk easily, and after storing my meager possessions in a locker box and making my bed, I went in search of Hoghead. It didn't take long to find him. I actually heard him before I saw him. Hoghead was in the TV area arguing with another prisoner about which team had won the first Super Bowl in 1967. I knew that it was Hoghead from Rooster's description - and because I heard the man arguing with him, shout, "Hoghead, you're outta your fuckin' mind! Ain't no way Green Bay won that game! Kansas City won! I remember it like it was yesterday 'cause I was with my first wife then, and I watched the game over at my father-in-law's house."

"You're a fuckin' idiot!" yelled Hoghead. "Green Bay won! The score was 35 to 10. I know 'cause I won a ten-dollar bet on that game. And asshole, I can even tell you who the coach was for Green Bay. It was Vince Lombardi. And I can tell you the date . . . January 15th. January fuckin' 15th! And the quarterback was Bart Starr! Bart fuckin' Starr! You probably don't even know who Bart Starr is. Now, don't try to tell me who won! I know who won!"

Standing to the side, I waited until the argument died down, then approached Hoghead. "What' up," I said to Hoghead, nodding my head.

'Don't know," said Hoghead cautious, as most prisoners are when a prisoner they don't know approaches them. "What's up with you."

"I was in the doghouse with Rooster. Just got out a coupla hours ago. He said to look you up when I got to pop."

"Yeah," said Hoghead, relaxing his guard. "How's he doin' up there?"

"He's makin' it. Only got a coupla' months left. I was in the cell next to 'im, the same cell Charlie was in."

"Oh," said Hoghead. "I hate Charlie died. We used to argue all the time, but Charlie was alright with me. Hated to see him go like that."

"They call me Troy."

"Hoghead," he said, shaking my hand. "Say, you know who won the first Super Bowl in 1967? This idiot's been tryin' to tell me Kansas City won, but I know Green Bay beat 'em that year."

"Man, I ain't got no idea," I said. "I don't even remember where I was in '67, probably in federal prison, best I can remember. Look, Rooster said that when you can, send him a coupla packs of smokes by that kitchen worker brings the trays up to the doghouse."

"Sure," said Hoghead. "I'll take care of it. What bed you on?"

"Bed eighty-two."

"I'm on forty-six. Holler at me you need anything."

"Sure thing," I said. "Talk to ya'."

Chapter Sixteen
Caveman

The dormitory was packed—a hundred-thirty men lived in a space that would have been crowded with seventy-five - but I was fortunate to get a bed next to a window, affording me a little more space. Assigned to the bed next to me was a man with a curious nickname. He politely waited until I had stowed my property and made my bed before introducing himself. "They call me Caveman," he said.

"Name's Troy," I said, extending my hand. "That your real name?"

"Real name's Hardy, but they been callin' me Caveman so long I'm used to it now."

"Rather be called Hardy?" I asked.

"Nah, Caveman's alright."

Caveman washed his face, then while brushing his teeth looked at himself in the mirror. He had never liked what he saw there but had learned to be okay with the image that stared back at him. As a child in elementary school he had often been the butt of jokes, and even more so in prison, where grown men with childish mentalities can be even more cruel than children. Bald, except for a crown of dark, brown, coarse hair ringing a head that looked as if it had been crafted out of clay by an amateur sculptor, he had long, bushy eyebrows; small, dark, almost black eyes; a broad nose; and large ears with a sprinkling of dark stubble. At five-ten, Caveman

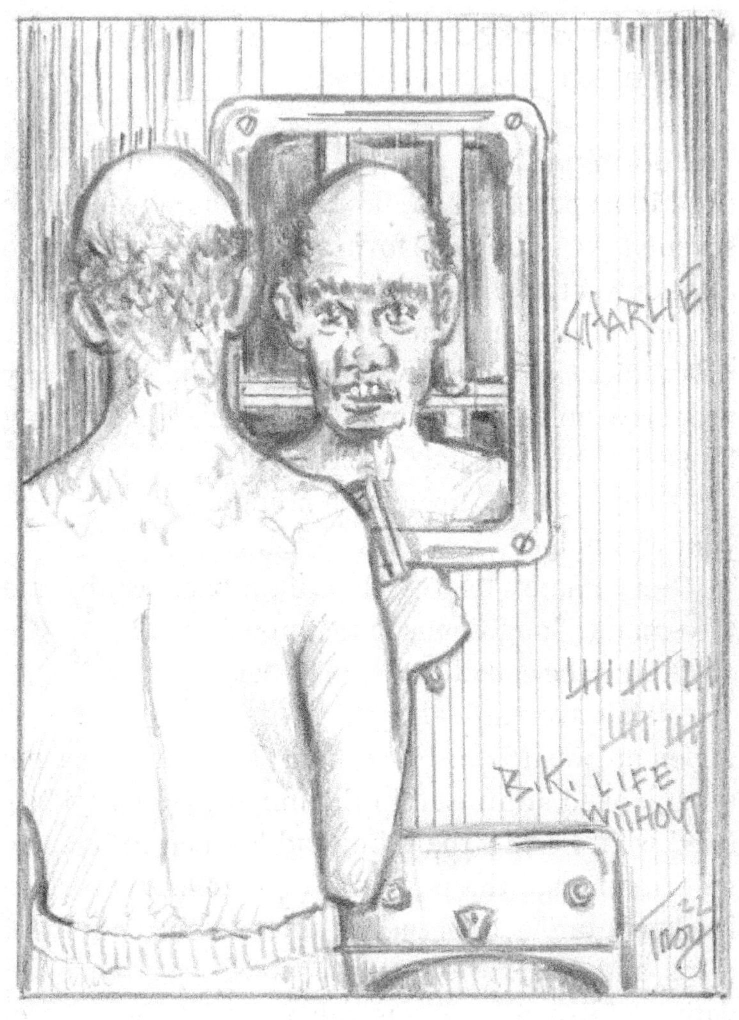

CHARLIE
UH UH UH
UH UH
B.K. LIFE
WITHOUT

weighed a lean one-sixty. He had a pot belly, and a slight hump in his back that caused him to walk stooped.

The son of sharecroppers, he grew up in extreme poverty in South Alabama during a time and place when more value was placed on the cultivation of cotton than education. So he learned to work hard but could barely read or write by the time he ran away from home at fifteen to drift and work temporary jobs.

The life of a drifter was adventurous, but lonely without the anchor of family and friends. Caveman quickly turned to drugs and alcohol to fill the void, then to petty crime to feed his newfound addictions. At eighteen, he was convicted of burglary and sentenced to two years in prison. There, like most young, angry, disillusioned first-time offenders, he left prison more angry than when he entered. Soon after his release, he found himself back in prison, this time with a ten-year sentence for drug possession.

Released seven years later, and now a seasoned convict and a committed criminal, Caveman's next arrest and conviction, only six months later, was for stealing a lawn mower. Judged a habitual offender at only twenty-eight, he was sentenced to life without parole.

Without hope, Caveman quickly immersed himself in the prison culture, always looking for the next high or distraction - anything to help numb the reality of spending the rest of his life in prison. He chased drugs and wasted his days talking to like-minded men about their past crimes or planning new ones should they ever see daylight again. Caveman, now forty, had been in prison twelve years, the last seven at Donaldson, where he worked as a baker in the prison's kitchen.

Chapter Seventeen
It's Just a Cup of Coffee

In an unfamiliar environment, and unable to sleep that first night, I stayed up late reading. About two a.m., when it was quiet and almost everyone in the dorm was asleep, I looked over the top of my book to see the old man, Jack, who had gotten out of the doghouse a couple weeks before me, walk past. Leaning on his cane for support, he was barefoot and naked, except for the dirty boxer shorts he wore. In his free hand he carried a small, round snuff can, and every few feet he stopped, looked down at the floor, then moved his cane around like a metal detector.

What's he doing? I strained to see. When I saw him stoop, pick something up, and put it in the can he carried, I understood. Cigarette butts. He's pickin' up cigarette butts. I went back to my book.

Early one morning a few days later, when Jack stopped near my bed to pick up a cigarette butt, I put my book aside and said, "Good mornin'." Jack paused and looked at me as if I had spoken a foreign language. "Good mornin'," I repeated.

"Ain't nothin' good 'bout it," mumbled Jack.

"Oh, I don't know," I said. "Least we woke up above ground this mornin'. I'd call that a good mornin'".

"Humph," grunted Jack.

"Say, you wanna cup of coffee?" I asked.

"Why?" asked Jack, cautiously.

"I don't know, just thought you might want one, that's all."

"Ain't got nothin' to give you for it," said Jack.

"Ain't askin' for nothin'. It's just a cup of coffee."

"Humph," said Jack. He turned and limped off.

I shook my head. Man, tryin' to get to know that old dude is like tryin' to make friends with a wild animal. I picked up my book and continued to read. A few minutes later, Jack returned. In his hand he held a dirty, coffee-stained plastic cup. He stepped closer and reached the cup toward me. I picked up a nearby jar of instant coffee and put a heaping spoon of coffee in the cup. Without a word Jack limped off.

The next morning, I awakened to find two small plastic containers of jelly on the wooden footlocker next to my bunk. Puzzled, I looked around, then noticed Jack standing on the other side of the dorm watching me. I understood. Picking up the containers of jelly, I saluted him. Carrying his coffee cup, Jack walked over, and again, without a word, thrust his cup at me. Again I gave him a spoon of coffee.

Every morning for the next two weeks, I awakened to find a small gift on my locker box. One day it was two rubber bands; another day, a pencil; then two Band-Aids; a couple paper clips; a biscuit; and once, a long, black crow's feather. And every morning Jack, without a word, came by for a spoon of coffee.

One morning, to my surprise, Jack sat down on the locker box next to my bed, took a sip of coffee, smacked his lips, and said, "It's a good mornin', ain't it."

"Yeah," I laughed, "it's a good mornin', alright."

"That's 'cause we woke up above ground, ain't that right," said Jack.

"Yep," I laughed again. "It's good 'cause we woke up above ground." And for the first time, I saw Jack grin, and it was like an unexpected ray of sunshine on a cloudy day.

So began a ritual that would last for the next two years. Every morning Jack and I sat together and sipped our coffee, usually in silence, each entertaining his own thoughts, but sometimes we talked. At first it was just small talk, the usual prisoner complaints about the living conditions; the harassment by the guards and oppression by the administration; his unfair conviction and sentence and such; but as trust grew between us (not insignificant in prison, where men often learn that trust ends in deceit and disappointment) we talked about our past, and our hopes and dreams (which were few), and our disappointments (which were many). And I discovered that this strange, bitter, little old man was so much more than the sum of his curious psychological traits and his physical limitations.

Jack was irascible, foul-mouthed, stubborn, and bigoted. In his mid-seventies, he had thin, white hair that spiked in all directions. Standing just five-four, he had short, bandy legs and claw-like, nicotine-stained fingers the color of an old meerschaum pipe. Toothless, he had a ruddy complexion and a vein-streaked, bulbous nose. His washed-out cornflower-blue eyes studied the world with either pained confusion or unyielding determination. He had been at Donaldson for over ten years, and was serving two life sentences for murder and attempted murder. Believing that he had been unjustly convicted and imprisoned, Jack refused to cooperate or follow the rules.

Born and raised in Birmingham, not thirty miles from Donaldson prison, Jack had been forced to work in his father's small junk business at an early age, seldom going to school. But he was far from stupid and quickly learned the art of bartering, and reading people. Studying their faces, body language, and even the tone of their voices, Jack always looked for an advantage and often found it. But like most people, Jack had serious character flaws: It was hard for him to trust anyone; he had little patience or tolerance; and he had even less self-control. One thing he had in abundance was an explosive temper, which often caused him to lose whatever advantage he may have gained.

When his father died, Jack took over his father's junk business, as well as the care of his mother, who was chronically ill and confined to a wheelchair.

The neighborhood where Jack grew up had always been poor but safe. Then in the late seventies, it began to change. What had once been a peaceful neighborhood slowly turned into an urban wasteland. Teens ran free at all hours, creating havoc and vandalizing property. Once-quiet streets became busy thoroughfares thronged with pimps, prostitutes, and roving gangs of drug dealers. Jack's house was burglarized. Gunshots often awakened him and his mother at night. Tools were stolen from his shop out back, and once, after Jack had confronted teens playing loud music and smoking pot in his front yard, someone threw a brick through his front window, almost hitting his mother who had been sitting in the living room watching TV. Jack called the police, but they ignored him.

One-night Jack got into a heated argument with a group of teens hanging out in his front yard. Threats and racial slurs were exchanged. When two of the teens climbed onto his front porch, Jack grabbed his father's old double-barreled shotgun and fired both barrels, killing one teen and seriously injuring the other.

After his arrest, Jack's court-appointed lawyer tried to get him to plea bargain for a lesser sentence, telling him that because the state didn't have a self-defense law he would probably get a life sentence if convicted, but Jack refused. He continued to insist that he was only protecting his life and property, and demanded a jury trial. He was quickly convicted and, at the age of sixty-five, was sentenced to two life terms in prison.

From the day Jack arrived at Donaldson, he refused to bathe, shave, cut, or even comb his hair. He also refused to wear shoes, a shirt, or even pants. He wouldn't sweep or mop his living area or make his bed, opting instead to sleep on an old, bare, plastic mattress, covering himself in winter with plastic trash bags and an old army blanket he had found in the trash. More than once, the guards, and even other prisoners, forced Jack into the shower. And over the years, he was repeatedly thrown into the doghouse for rule infractions, but nothing and nobody could make Jack obey. Finally, everybody just gave up and ignored the strange old man, treating him as if he didn't exist.

A month after I was released from the doghouse, I was assigned a job in the prison library, a job I had wanted for years. The job gave me an opportunity to get first crack at the new books when they arrived. Of course, most of the time they were used books, but they were new to me. My job was to deliver books to those prisoners confined on Death Row, in the doghouse, and as patients in the infirmary. Remembering what it was like to spend time in lockup without anything to read, I took the job seriously.

I soon developed a routine: I got up at six a.m., drank a cup of coffee with Jack, then sat on my bunk reading until I went to work in the library at seven-thirty. I usually left the library around four p.m. every day, then worked out, took a shower, read again until around nine, and finally went to sleep.

Chapter Eighteen
Rooster Gets Out Too

Rooster got out of the doghouse Thursday evening, and the shakedown squad hit the dormitory early Friday morning.

At three a.m. all the lights in the dorm were suddenly turned on, and twelve correctional officers, all dressed in black and carrying pepper spray and long batons, rushed through the front door, shouting. The lead guard aimed a shotgun loaded with rubber bullets at the ceiling and fired - the sound, as intended, startling and scaring all of us. All, that is, except Jack.

"Everybody on the fuckin' floor, now!" shouted Captain Rankhart. "Let's go! Hit the floor, face down, hands on top of your head, ankles locked!"

The guards moved in between the beds, yelling, "Move! Move! On the floor, face down! Move!" Those prisoners not responding fast enough (except Jack, who stayed on his bed and was ignored) were pulled from their bunks and forced onto the floor.

At the sound of the shotgun I rolled off my bunk and onto the floor. Face down, my hands on top of my head, and ankles crossed as instructed, I turned my face a little to one side and tried to see what was happening. When a guard saw me looking around, he walked over, straddled me, and pushed my face into the concrete. "Face down!" He yelled. "I said, face down! Don't move!"

"I can't breathe with my face in the concrete," I mumbled.

"What'd you say, smartass!" asked the guard. I didn't answer. He turned his attention to another prisoner a few feet away.

The shakedown took about three hours. One by one, we were stripped naked and searched. Then wearing only boxer shorts, we were rushed outside to sit on the blacktop in orderly rows, our hands positioned on top of our heads, while the dormitory was carefully searched.

Once back inside, we found our living area a shambles: the TV benches were overturned; the tables were upside-down; the three plastic trash cans had been emptied onto the floor; and our mattresses, sheets, blankets, photos and personal papers were all mixed together, strewn from one end of the dorm to the other. Chaos ensued as prisoners searched for their personal property. It took the rest of the day to clean up and put things back to normal.

Later, I sat with Rooster and Hoghead on a bench in the TV area. "Must of heard you was getting' out and figured they'd better find all the contraband before you hit population," Hoghead said to Rooster.

"Hell, I ain't been out long enough to get my hands on no contraband yet," said Rooster. "Only been out 'bout twelve hours. You lose anything?" he asked me.

"Didn't have much. Just an extra pillow and a plastic water bottle. They got that, but that ain't nothin' I can't get my hands on again."

"That's what we do," said Rooster. It's like a fuckin' game with these assholes. We spend months collectin' the shit we need to make life livable in this hellhole, then they come along every so often, shake us down and take it. Then we start collectin' the same shit all over again." He changed gears. "Say, I see that dude Caveman sleeps next to you."

"Yeah, he seems alright. Don't bother nobody."

"He's a little strange, but he's alright," Rooster said, nodding his head in agreement. "Me and Hoghead used to sell him pot when I was in population last time. He still workin' in the kitchen?"

"Yeah. He's at work now."

"He's an ugly bastard, but that son of a bitch can bake his ass off. Makes the best rolls and cornbread I ever ate in prison. And his cinnamon rolls! Man, they melt in your mouth. He ever tell you how he got the name Caveman?"

"Nah, I never asked him."

"It was that young dude Jerry gave him the handle, and it stuck. We was watchin' a ball game on TV and this commercial came on for Geico insurance. They had a caveman dressed like a tennis player and the announcer comes on and says something like 'So easy, even a caveman can do it.' And I swear, that caveman in the commercial was the spittin' image of Caveman. Looked just like him. Coulda been his twin brother. That's when Jerry yelled, 'Hey, they got Hardy on TV doin' commercials!' Everybody in the TV area turned to look at Hardy and laughed their asses off. 'I'm gonna start callin' you Caveman,' said Jerry, and the name stuck. Everybody started callin' him Caveman from that day on. He's alright. You could do worse for a bunk partner."

"Yeah, he's alright. Don't talk much, which is okay with me," I said.

"I see Old Man Jack's livin' in Two Dorm too," said Rooster.

"Yeah, I kinda like that old dude," I said. "Me and him drink coffee most mornin's. I guess I feel a little sorry for 'im too, and I guess I call myself lookin' out for 'im. You gotta admit he got a raw deal in court. I mean he admits that he shot those two teenagers, but seems to me it was really self-defense, seein' as he was just protectin' his property."

"Hell, you ask me, we all got a raw deal," said Rooster. "But there's one thing about Jack you gotta watch out for."

"What's that?" I asked.

"Well, a lot of times he says and does things without thinking, so you gotta be careful he don't get you in a bad situation, know what I mean."

Just a few weeks after he got out of the doghouse, Rooster finagled a way to get assigned as the trash man - a job that may not seem desirable to people in the society, but in prison it's a prestigious job because it allows you to move freely, and being able to move about freely inside a maximum-security facility can be very lucrative, especially if one is open to moving contraband from point A to point B. And Rooster was always eager to find a way to make a dollar.

Chapter Nineteen
There Ain't No Santa

Sitting on my bed the first Christmas I knew Jack, I put two packs of tobacco and a bag of instant coffee in a small brown, paper bag, carefully rolled the bag into a tube and taped it. With a magic marker I wrote To Jack, From Santa on the bag.

Walking over to Jack's bed, I placed the paper bag on top of an old coat that Jack used for a pillow. An hour later, when Jack returned from the infirmary and walked past my bed, I cheerfully said, "Merry Christmas, Jack."

"Humph," said Jack, barely pausing before continuing to his bed.

From my bed I watched Jack, preparing to enjoy the change in attitude I expected to see when he found the gift I'd left him.

But when Jack saw the paper bag on his bed, he was far from joyful. Instead, he shouted, "I told you sumbitches to stay away from my bed, dammit!" Using his cane like a sword, Jack raked the bag onto the floor; then using it like a golf club, he swung at the paper bag. It slid across the concrete floor and hit a nearby wall.

"What set Jack off?" Caveman asked me. He had also witnessed Jack's outburst.

"Man, I don't know," I said. "All I did was put some tobacco and coffee in a paper bag and put it on his bed. Thought he'd be happy when he found it, but instead he freaked out."

"You left a paper bag on his bed!"

"Yeah. Had tobacco and coffee in it."

"Well, that explains it. No wonder he freaked out," said Caveman.

"Explains what? What're you talkin' about?"

"Well, a couple years ago, Jack came back from chow one day and found this paper bag on his bed. And when he opened it, he found shit smeared inside it. You should'a seen 'im. Man, he went fuckin' crazy. Cussed everybody out in the dorm, wouldn't talk to nobody for a coupla weeks."

"Who the hell would do somethin' like that?" I asked.

"Nobody owned up to it, but if I had to guess, it was probably that young dude, Jerry, the dude Jack hit with his cane. He's always playin' tricks on Jack."

"Man, that's dirty," I said. "Well, let me go see if I can calm 'im down."

I walked over to Jack's bed, where he sat rolling a cigarette. "What's wrong, Jack? What you yellin' about?"

"That!" shouted Jack, pointing his cane at the battered paper bag on the floor. "Some sumbitch put a sack of shit on my bed!"

I walked over, picked up the paper bag, brought it back and sat down on Jack's bed. "You talkin' 'bout this?"

"Get it away from me!" shouted Jack. "It's got shit in it!"

"How you know? You ain't even opened it to see what's inside."

"I just know. It's like that other time. They tryin' to trick me."

I sniffed the bag. "Smells okay to me. Here, you smell it." I reached the bag toward Jack.

"No!" yelled Jack, leaning back. "It's a trick! I know it! They tryin' to trick me!"

"Look Jack, I been tricked a time or two myself, so I know how it feels, but this don't look like no trick to me. "While Jack closely watched, I squeezed the bag, turning it over and over in my hands, the expression on Jack's face telling me that he expected the bag to burst open at any moment and cover his bed in shit. "Look, Jack, I ain't the smartest man in the world, not even the smartest man in this prison, but I've learned over the years that sometimes in life you just gotta take a chance and trust somebody, even if it don't make no sense. Sometimes you just gotta step out into the deep water. Know what I mean. You can't stay in knee-high water all your life. Sometimes you just gotta take a deep breath and swim out to the deep end."

"I can't even swim," said Jack.

"Dammit, Jack!" I said, losing my patience. "I ain't really talkin' 'bout swimmin'! I'm talkin' 'bout trustin' somebody."

"Then, why don't you just say that," said Jack. "You the one talkin' 'bout swimmin'."

I sighed. "Okay, Jack, let me just say this clear so you'll understand me. I know for a fact this bag ain't got shit in it. Here, take it," I said, extending the bag toward him again.

Jack put his hands behind his back. "No! I know it's a trick! They tryin' to trick me!"

"Jack, who's tryin' to trick you?"

"Them dudes don't like me. They tryin' to trick me."

"Jack, you ain't got no earthly idea who put this bag on your bed." I turned the bag over. "Look, here." I held the bag up so that Jack could see what was written on it. "It says To Jack, From Santa. Now, how 'bout that. Looks like Santa's the one put this bag on your bed."

"There ain't no Santa," said Jack.

"Damn, Jack. Why you gotta' make everything so difficult. Come on - 'course we both know there ain't no real Santa. Santa's just an idea somebody came up with, just a reason for family and friends to get together once a year and show their love and appreciation by givin' each other gifts. Santa's all about kindness and appreciation and trust. Understand?"

Jack nodded his head yes. Okay, I thought. Now I'm finally starting to get somewhere. "So, how about trustin' a friend." Once more I held the bag toward him. Again, Jack stepped back, as if I had tried to hand him a rattlesnake.

Frustrated, I ripped the tape off the bag, but when I attempted to dump the contents onto Jack's bed, Jack grabbed my arm. "Nooo!" he yelled. But before he could stop me, out tumbled two packs of tobacco and a shiny red bag of instant coffee. Jack's eyes grew as big as silver dollars. He reached out and caressed the bag of coffee and the two packs of tobacco, then looked up at me, an impish grin on his scraggly, old face. Jack chuckled, "Heh. Heh." Then he whispered, "Santa."

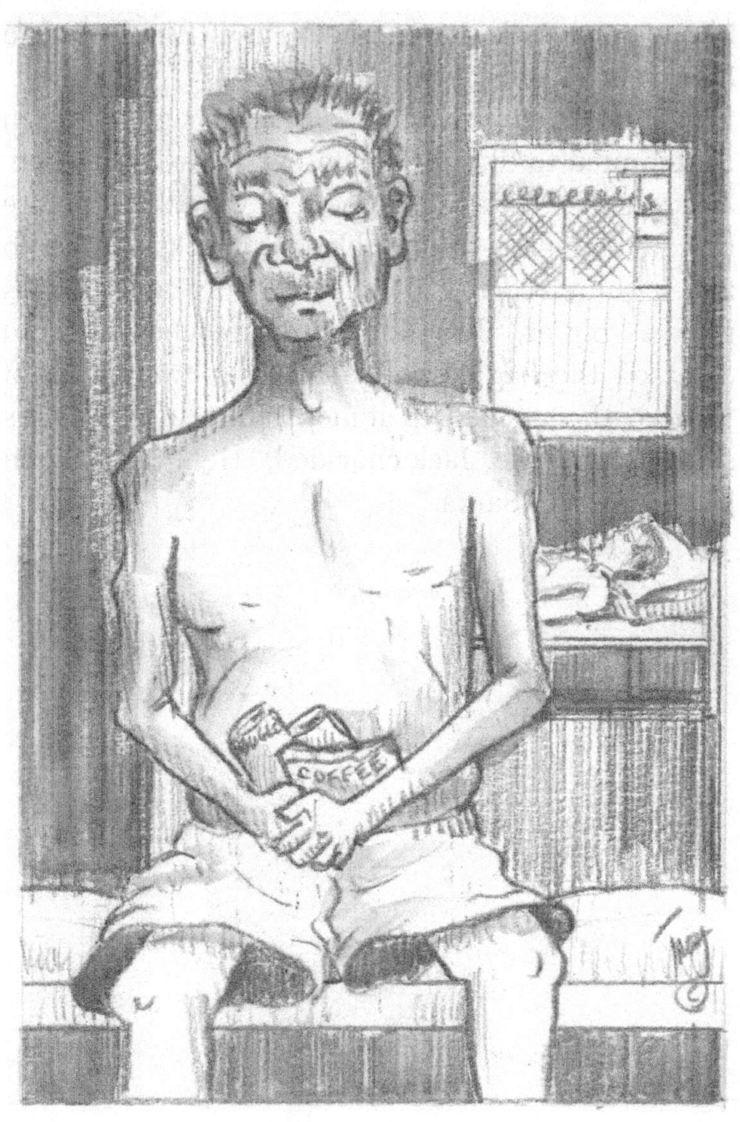

COFFEE

Chapter Twenty
Jack's Sit-Down Strike

Jack had severe diabetes, and not long after Christmas his legs began to swell, making it difficult for him to get from his bunk to the toilet, to the chow hall, or up the long hall to the infirmary for his daily shot of insulin. Repeatedly he asked, first the nurses, then the doctor, for a wheelchair, but his requests were ignored.

Jack's problem troubled me. One day while talking to Rooster I had an idea. "How you like your job pushin' the trash cart?" I asked.

"It's alright, it's a job. Kind of a hassle, though, pickin' up trash three times a day, seven days a week, but every once in a while I'll run up on somethin' and make me a little hustle."

"I was just thinkin', since you gotta go that way anyway, how 'bout lettin' Jack ride on your cart as far as the infirmary. You know he can't hardly walk, and they won't give him a wheelchair. And he needs to get up there every day so he can get his insulin shot."

"Hell, that ain't no problem," said Rooster. "You tell him all he gotta do is hop on when I get ready to go and I'll push 'em up there, drop 'im off right outside the door."

Most prisoners at Donaldson knew that Jack was having difficulty walking and that he had been denied a wheelchair. They also knew how strange and stubborn he was, so few were surprised when they saw him ride past on the trash cart, a large, open, flatbed wagon with hard rubber tires. They waved and cheered for Jack - a hero that had figured out how to beat the system. And Jack loved the attention. He played the part too, sitting atop the large, plastic bags of trash like a king on a Mardi Gras float, head erect, legs splayed, a lit cigarette dangling from his lips, one hand on his cane, and the other free, waving at those he favored (who were few) and snubbing those he didn't (who were many).

Jack's audacious behavior inspired the rebellious, stimulated the imagination of the dispirited, and unfortunately, antagonized and embarrassed the guards and the prison administration. When the warden heard of Jack's seditious behavior, he vowed to put an end to it.

One day, Jack, after getting his insulin shot, was sitting on a bench in the infirmary waiting for Rooster to return with the trash cart when a guard told him, "You're gonna have to make your way back to your living area the best you can, 'cause the warden told me to tell you that you can't ride on that trash cart no more." Without a word, Jack got up, limped over to the cubicle where the infirmary guard worked, found a spot on the floor and sat down, refusing to move.

The news of Jack's sit-down strike in the infirmary traveled quickly throughout the prison. When I told Rooster about it, he offered to walk up to the infirmary with me to see if we could persuade Jack to give up a battle we were sure he couldn't win, and one that would probably end badly.

We found Jack sitting on the floor next to the cubicle. "Come on, Jack," I said. "Get up and let me and Rooster help you back to the dorm."

"I ain't gettin' up," said Jack. "I weren't hurtin' nobody ridin' up here on Rooster's buggy, and I'm gonna stay right here 'til they get me a wheelchair."

"Let 'im stay, he wants," said Rooster. "At least he won't have far to go to get his insulin shot. Tell you the truth, I'm surprised they ain't already called the goon squad to come up here and drag his ass off to the doghouse. If it was me or you up here protestin', they woulda' already kicked our ass and put us in the doghouse."

"Probably so," I said, "but Jack's old and it wouldn't look too good for 'em to beat up on an old man, least not in front of all these nurses, doctors, and free-world people they got workin' here. Anyway, they figure he'll give up soon enough."

"I ain't givin' up!" shouted Jack, overhearing me. "It just ain't fair. I weren't hurtin' nobody ridin' on that cart and I ain't leavin'!"

"I'll tell you what, Jack," I said, "let me and Rooster help you back to the dorm, and I'll go talk to the woman runs the infirmary myself, see if I can talk her into gettin' you a wheelchair. How 'bout that."

"No! She ain't gonna' do nothin'. I'm gonna' stay here 'til I get me a wheelchair," said Jack.

"Damn, Jack! I ain't never met nobody stubborn as you," I said, throwing up my hands, disgusted. "Well, alright, then, if you've made up your mind, I give up tryin' to talk you out of it. I'll be back to check on you this evenin'."

Later, Rooster, Hoghead, and I sat on my bed talking. "Man, I can't believe Jack's so hardheaded. Was he like that on the streets?" I asked Hoghead.

"Pretty much the same," said Hoghead. "I didn't know 'im all that good, but I used to run into 'im every once in a while. Me and him used to both sell scrap iron to a place in Bessemer, not too far from here. But there's one thing I do remember about 'im, and that's if he thought you was tryin' to take advantage of 'im or cheat 'im out of a dime for his scrap, he'd drive a hundred miles outta the way and sell it somewhere else, even if he had to take a loss. When Jack thinks he's right, to hell with everything - he won't budge an inch. I knew Jack's old man, too, before he passed away, and he was the same way, stubborn as a mule. Guess Jack got it from him."

"He's a stubborn bastard, ain't no doubt," said Rooster. He turned to me. "And remember, I told you, if you ain't careful, Old Man Jack's gonna get you in some shit."

"You got that right," said Hoghead.

"I ain't worried 'bout it," I said. "But you gotta admire him for stickin' to his guns. Not many in here would buck the system like he does."

"Most ain't got the guts," said Hoghead.

"Or crazy enough," said Rooster.

That evening after supper, carrying a small package of cigarettes and coffee, I went to the infirmary to check on Jack and was surprised to find him still there. I had expected to hear that he had been forcibly removed and was now in the doghouse. But there he was, on the floor, lying on a bed he had fashioned of his old coat. "Here," I said, handing him the coffee and cigarettes. "How long you gonna camp out here?"

"I weren't hurtin' nobody ridin' on Rooster's cart."

"Shit, I know that, Jack, but that's just how it is in prison. Problem was you looked like you was havin' too much fun, like you was thumbin' your nose at 'em, and the warden didn't like that. And what the warden says here at Donaldson is law. He makes the rules."

"Well, they ain't my rules. I ain't suppose to be here anyway. I was just tryin' to take care of my mama and my house, that's all. His rules ain't my rules."

At that moment, Mrs. Chamberlain, the infirmary administrator, walked past, obviously leaving for the day. I saw an opportunity to talk to her.

"Hold it a minute," I said to Jack. "That's the lady runs the infirmary. Let me go see if I can talk to her."

"She ain't gonna' do nothin'," said Jack.

"Never know 'til you try," I said, hurrying to catch up with her.

"Excuse me. Can I speak to you a few minutes?" I asked the administrator.

She paused and turned, one hand on the door. "I was just leaving." She sighed. "It's been a long day."

"I promise I won't take long, just a few minutes."

"Okay, but make it quick, please," she said, brushing her hand through her short brown hair and adjusting her round wire glasses.

"You see, I'm a friend of Jack's," I said, turning to look at Jack thirty feet away.

"I'm aware of the situation," she said. "I thought he would have left by now."

"That's just it, he can't leave. He can't walk but a few steps. That's why he needs a wheelchair real bad."

"I understand, I really do and I'd like to help, but unfortunately we just don't have any more chairs available right now."

"Well, what if I could find somebody willing to donate a wheelchair for him to use?" I asked.

"I'm sorry," said the administrator, "and I do appreciate your concern for your friend, but prison policy expressly forbids private donations for the personal use of inmates."

"I didn't know that."

"Well, I'm sure you can see what that could lead to."

Even though I had spent years trying to control my emotions, especially when talking to those in authority, I slipped for a moment, and in frustration raised my voice, "Even if that inmate can't hardly walk! How's he supposed to get to the bathroom or the chow hall . . . or up here to get his insulin!"

"Well, that is a problem," she said. "But we just don't have an extra wheelchair we can give him right now. I wish we did - that would make everything so much easier for everybody." She turned to look at Jack. "I'm sorry."

"I am too," I said, an edge to my voice. I paused, then said more calmly, "Thanks for your time." The infirmary administrator turned and left.

Jack spent the night sleeping on the floor of the infirmary. The next morning the warden told one of his guards, "I want you to go tell the convict that pushes the trash cart to go up to the infirmary and get that old man sitting on the floor there. Tell him to take him back to his dormitory and drop him off." Then, the warden gave the guard further instructions.

When the trash cart stopped at the infirmary and Rooster told Jack that he had been told to come get him, Jack was delighted. With Rooster's help, Jack gladly climbed onto the trash cart.

Rooster and Jack were met by a guard near the entrance to the dormitory. As instructed, the guard patiently waited until Rooster helped Jack off the cart, then told them, "I got a message for both of you from the warden." He turned to Rooster. "He said to tell you that if you ever use this cart again for anything but hauling trash, he's gonna lock you up in the doghouse." He turned to Jack. "And you. He said you better not put your old ass on this cart again, 'cause if you do he's gonna put you in the doghouse too." The guard turned and walked away.

"I knowed they was gonna' trick me! I knowed it!" fumed Jack. "Them sumbitches!"

Chapter Twenty-One
Gangrene

The next day, Jack was given a brand new wheelchair, and he was as surprised and happy as a kid finding a new bicycle under the Christmas tree.

I was the only person Jack would let touch his wheelchair. When Hoghead offered to push him to the chow hall, Jack told him, "Hell no! That takes all the fun outta it. I can push myself."

And what fun Jack had, much to the misery of everyone. He quickly realized that it was easier to push his wheelchair backward, using his bare, swollen feet on the dirty concrete floor, rather than forward using his frail arms. The only problem was that to travel backward, he had to look over his shoulder, and sometimes he forgot to do so, creating havoc in the crowded dormitory: Jack jammed the doorway, rammed into walls, hit tables and chairs, and ran over the feet of other prisoners sitting on the edge of their bunks.

"You mowin' down half the prison with that wheelchair of yours," I joked. "Maybe we oughta go over to the maintenance shop and get 'em to put a rear view mirror and horn on that contraption."

"Heh. Heh," said Jack, clearly pleased with himself. "Them sumbitches just need to get outta the way they see me comin'."

In the chow hall, trying to balance his food tray on his lap, while slowly propelling his wheelchair

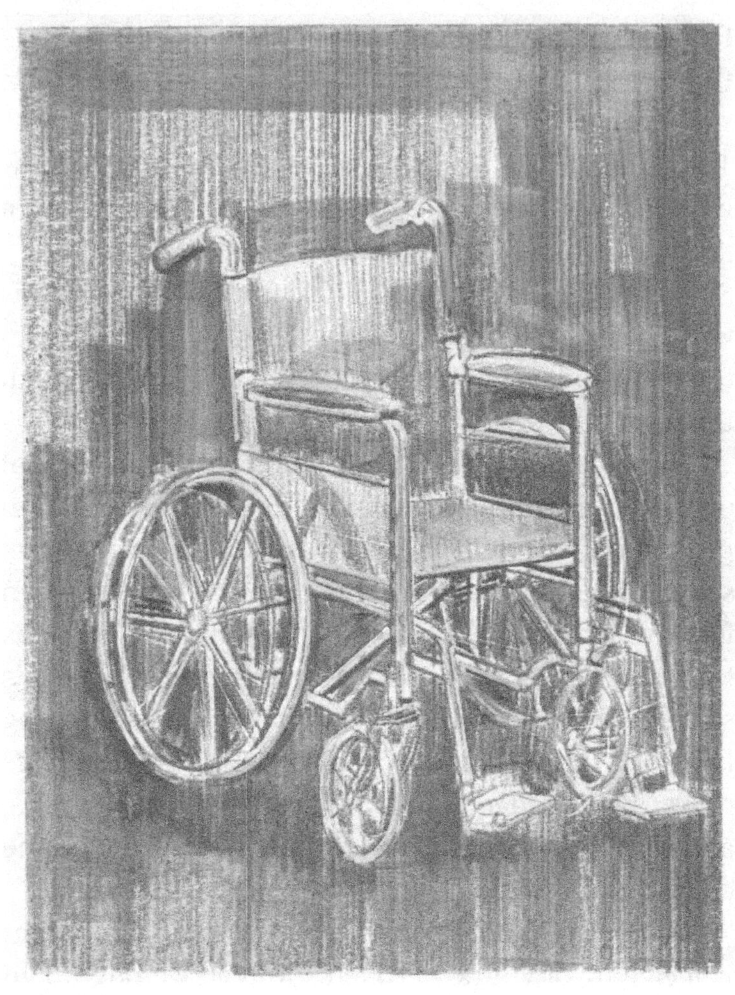

backwards, Jack held up the serving line, infuriating hungry and impatient convicts. When the prisoners openly complained and threatened Jack, I convinced him that it would be much easier and faster if he just maneuvered his wheelchair over to a table and waited while I went through the line and got trays for both of us.

A couple months after he got his wheelchair, a lesion appeared on top of Jack's right foot, and his foot swelled to twice its normal size. At the infirmary his foot was scrubbed clean, swabbed with ointment and wrapped in gauze. Jack was then instructed to keep it clean and to report to the infirmary every other day for a dressing change, but he ignored the medical advice, refusing to go to the infirmary while continuing to push his wheelchair with his feet, dragging his bandaged foot on the dirty concrete floor.

One day I noticed how the skin just above the filty bandage on Jack's foot was red and swollen. "Jack, it looks like to me that your foot's gettin' infected. Let me take a look at it," I told him.

"It's okay. It don't hurt no more."

"Maybe so, but let me take a look at it."

"I don't feel nothin'."

"I don't know if that's good or bad, Jack. When was the last time you went up to the infirmary and had that dressin' changed?"

"It don't need changin'. It don't hurt."

"Well, if it don't hurt, then it don't matter if I take a look at it."

"I don't want nobody messin' with it."

"Dammit Jack! Why you gotta be so stubborn!"

"'Cause it's my foot and it don't hurt!"

I tried a different approach. "Look, I'll tell you what. You just sit there and I'll fix us both a big cup of coffee and get you a cigarette to go with it. That way, you can just sit back and relax, drink your coffee, and smoke, while I take that nasty bandage off and look at it. How's that sound?"

"You gonna make the coffee strong?"

"You know it, just the way you like it. Now, gimme your cup and I'll be right back."

When I returned with the coffee, I handed Jack his cup, then sat on his bed. "Prop your foot up here on the edge of the mattress," I said. Jack, who was sitting in his wheelchair beside his bed did so.

While Jack smoked his cigarette and drank his coffee, I carefully removed the tape. When I unwrapped the gauze, layer upon layer of bluish-black skin came off with it. Jack's foot looked like a chunk of the red, raw meat one often sees displayed in a butcher shop window. The foul odor made me gag. "Damn, Jack! Your skin's peelin' off and pus is comin' out too. Man, this looks bad, real bad. Must hurt like hell."

"It don't hurt. Look," said Jack. And before I could stop him, Jack reached over and stuck his burning cigarette to the top of his foot. The raw skin sizzled like bacon in a hot frying pan and gave off the distinctive smell of burnt flesh.

"Dammit, Jack! Are you fuckin' crazy! Look at the blister you just burned on top of your foot!"

"Heh. Heh," chuckled Jack, taking a sadistic pleasure at my reaction. "I told you, I can't feel nothin'. See." Again, he reached toward his foot with the lit cigarette, but this time I slapped the cigarette out of his hand. It landed on the floor and I stepped on it.

Enraged, Jack yelled, "You sumbitch! You took my cigarette! You sumbitch!"

"Damn right I took it!" I shouted. "If you're gonna' act like a damn fool, you don't need to smoke! I'll tell you what, Jack, I'm gonna push you up to the infirmary right now!"

"I don't wanna go to the infirmary!" Jack wailed like a child. "I ain't goin'!"

"Oh, you're goin', alright!" I shouted. Then, struggling to regain self-control, I lowered my voice and tried to reason with the stubborn old man. "Look, Jack. Your foot's messed up real bad. The skin's turnin' black and peelin' off. And you ain't got no feelin' in it. Now, I ain't no doctor, but from what I've read, this could be gangrene. And you could lose you whole foot. It might even kill you if you don't get it treated right away."

"I ain't goin' to the infirmary. I ain't got no gang greed."

"Don't you want your foot to get better?"

"They'll make me stay up there, I know it."

"But you might need to. Least 'til your foot gets better."

"They won't let me smoke up there."

"I can't believe what I'm hearin', I said, genuinely astonished. "Here, your foot's rottin' off, and all you're worried about is smokin'." I grabbed the handles of Jack's wheelchair and spun it around. "Let's go!" I shouted.

Jack pouted and wouldn't speak to me during the trip to the infirmary. The doctor there examined Jack's foot and immediately admitted him to the ward. The next day I heard that Jack had been rushed to a free-world hospital for treatment.

Every few days I asked at the infirmary about Jack's condition, but no one seemed to know. Finally, one morning, a couple weeks later, one of the guards that worked there told me that he had heard that Jack's leg had been amputated and that he had died of infection.

I felt stunned with sadness and guilt, and told Caveman, "I hate it that the last time me and Jack talked, we argued, and hell, Caveman, if I had known he was gonna die anyway, I would have just left him alone, instead makin' him go the infirmary. Then he coulda stayed around his friends and smoked all he wanted, instead of spendin' his last days around all them strangers, all the time cravin' a cigarette."

That's just it," said Caveman, "ain't no way you could know Jack was gonna' die. You just did what you thought was the right thing."

Chapter Twenty-Two
Resurrection

Two weeks later, I was working in the library when Rooster came by. "You ain't gonna believe this," he said.

"I don't believe half the shit I hear at Donaldson?"

"Guess who they just brought in the back gate?"

"I give. Who? Somebody I know?"

"Oh, you know him, alright," said Rooster.

"Well, who is it?"

"Jack!"

"You're shittin' me! I thought Jack was dead!"

"I guess he done come back to life!" chuckled Rooster. "'Cause I just saw him when I was pushin' the trash to the back gate. And that's gospel. I was at the back gate unloadin' the trash cart and this van pulls into the sally port. And when they open the side door, out pops Jack big as life. He was missin' a leg but it was him alright. They took him up to the infirmary."

The next day Jack was released from the infirmary and sent back to the dormitory.

Every Tuesday at six o'clock, Jack telephoned his mother at the nursing home where she now lived, and for Jack it was the most important event in his life. Since he hadn't been able to call her while he was in the free-world hospital, that first Tuesday back, Jack eagerly - but now more slowly with only one leg - made his way over to the dormitory's bank of wall-mounted telephones . I watched from my bed as a frustrated Jack dialed the phone, held for a moment, then dialed again and again. I walked over to see if I could help. "What's wrong, Jack?" I asked.

"Them sumbitches won't take my call," whined Jack. "Nobody's pickin' up. It's six o'clock and I always call my mama at six on Tuesday."

"Sure you dialed the right number?"

Jack showed me a crumpled piece of paper with a phone number written on it. "This here's her number. I called the number on this here paper."

"You want me to try?" I asked. Jack handed me the piece of paper and I carefully dialed three times, but every time the call was refused. "Don't know what the problem is, Jack. Maybe we can try again tomorrow."

"But it's Tuesday. I always call on Tuesday."

"Could be the nursin' home's phone is messed up. Want me to push you back to your bed?"

"No. I'm gonna' stay right here 'til I talk to my mama."

"Jack, if the phone ain't workin', it ain't workin'. You keep dialin' ain't gonna' make it work."

"It's Tuesday, and I'm callin' my mama," insisted Jack.

"Okay, I give up," I said. "Need any help, holler." I walked back to my bed and sat down.

Jack sat at the phone for over an hour, stubbornly calling the phone number over and over. Finally, he gave up and made his way back to his bed.

All the next day, Jack moped around, and when I tried to cheer him up, he finally confided, " I'm just worried about my mama. She's the only one cares about me."

"That's not true, Jack. A lot of people care about you."

"Not like my mama. Ain't nobody ever gonna care about me like my mama does."

I couldn't argue with that, so I just let it be.

A couple days later, the chaplain sent for Jack, and I pushed him up the hall to the prison chapel. There, the chaplain told Jack that his mother had died while he was in the hospital.

"I know she ain't dead," said Jack, refusing to accept the news. "You're a liar and you're tryin' to trick me. I know my mama ain't dead! I just know it!"

As the days passed, Jack spoke less and less. He seldom went to the chow hall and began to lose weight. Every night, Jack parked his wheelchair in a corner facing the wall, and with a large towel draped over his head and shoulders, sat there until first light. And, exactly at six, every Tuesday for the next couple weeks, Jack worked his wheelchair over to the bank of telephones and sat, as if expecting his mother to call him.

Chapter Twenty-Three
The First Cold Wind

A month later, an event occurred that helped Jack accept the reality of his mother's death, deal with his grief, and restore him, not just to his old self, but to a better rendition of himself.

The first cold wind of autumn blew through Donaldson like an outbound freight, catching me and Jack ill-prepared when we left the chow hall that evening. "Whew!" I said, hunching my shoulders. "That wind's bitin'!"

"Sumbitch!" said Jack, reaching up to pull his knit cap over his ears. "I need me a cup of hot coffee."

"Don't worry, I'll fix us one when we get back to the dorm," I said, glad to see Jack taking an interest in life, even if it was for something as simple as a cup of coffee.

As we neared the dormitory we surprised dozens of goldfinch feeding on a small patch of grass out front. The birds rose up as one and took flight, their sudden movement and bright yellow color surprising and exciting Jack. "Just look at them little yeller birds!" exclaimed Jack. "Ain't they somethin'."

"Sure are," I said. "You see how they all took off at the same time. Like them synchronized swimmers you see at the Olympics. Must be at least a hundred or so. Come down here from up north somewhere to get away from the cold. Yeah, they're somethin', alright. I ain't never seen so many in one place."

"What you think they eat?" asked Jack.

"Oh, I don't know. I imagine they eat worms, bugs, probably some grass seed, anything they can find."

Inside the dorm, Jack worked his wheelchair over to the window beside my bed so that he could watch the little birds, now resettled on the same patch of grass.

The next evening the chow hall served the usual fare for midweek: cornbread; processed liver patty; collard greens; black-eyed peas, and rice. (Liver patties were one of the least-favorite meats at Donaldson. The prisoners disliked them so much that whenever they were served, they threw them on the floor in protest).

"You gonna eat that cornbread?" Jack asked.

"You still hungry?" I asked. Jack didn't answer. "Here," I handed him my cornbread. "Want the liver patty too?"

"Yeah," said Jack.

"If you can eat that liver patty, you're a better man than me, Jack," I joked, but Jack didn't respond. Instead he carefully wrapped the bread and meat in toilet paper and put it in his coat pocket.

"Ready to go?" I asked.

"Yep," said Jack.

I grabbed the handles of Jack's wheelchair, spun the chair around and headed for the exit, rolling over dozens of liver patties. When we neared the dormitory, once again we startled the little yellow birds, and again they rose to the sky as one. Jack insisted we stop to watch. He then asked me to park his wheelchair in the center of the small patch of grass where the birds had been feeding and to leave him there.

"You sure?" I asked. "It's kinda cold out here."

"I just wanna sit here for a spell," said Jack.
"Fine, I'm gonna get outta this wind." I said, and went inside.

About ten minutes later, I looked out the window and what I saw made me smile. Dozens of birds had encircled Jack's wheel- chair and were feeding on the crumbled cornbread he had spread around his chair. More and more landed as I watched.

Jack sat outside feeding and watching the birds until a guard approached him at sunset and told him that it was time to go inside. Inside, an excited Jack asked me, "Did ya' see 'em? Did ya' see all them little yeller birds? I was feedin' 'em."

"Yeah, I saw 'em, Jack. I was watchin' through the window."

"I charmed 'em with that cornbread."

"You sure did. Probably ruined them for grass seed and bugs."

"They didn't like that liver patty though," mused Jack.

"Well, them some smart birds," I said. " Ain't nothin' alive can digest one of them fuckin' liver patties."

The welfare of the goldfinches became Jack's new obsession, and he was determined to make the birds' lives as comfortable as possible. Directed by Jack, I wired two, small, round snuff cans to the fence separating the small patch of grass from the much larger recreation yard, filling one with crumpled cornbread and the other with water. Every day, after supper, Jack parked his wheelchair on the small patch of grass and fed the birds any food he had managed to smuggle out of the chow hall that day.

Watching Jack feed the birds in the evening quickly became a form of entertainment, not only for Jack, but for a small group of prisoners at Donaldson. Most evenings they gathered just outside the entrance to the dorm, sat or leaned against the building, smoked hand-rolled cigarettes, and talked while watching Jack feed the birds. And any newcomer to the group quickly learned the ground rules: no loud talking or noise; no sudden movement; and no getting too close to the birds while they were being fed. Transgressors were promptly reprimanded.

Jack, who up until that time had been an outcast and an object of ridicule at Donaldson, was now, through his careful treatment of the birds, treated with respect. Prisoners who had never spoken to him before now freely approached him as an authority on the care of birds. Often, they offered food or volunteered assistance. The old man had never felt so important.

"You know Jack, I was thinkin' you might be upsettin' the natural order of things by takin' such good care of those birds of yours," I joked. "Looks to me they may be gettin' so fat they might not be able to fly back up north come spring."

"Heh. Heh," chuckled Jack. "I'm feedin' 'em good, ain't I."

"Maybe too good. They might just stay here year 'round."

"If they do, I'll take care of 'em."

"I know you will."

Chapter Twenty-Four
Ya Kilt 'Im

A couple of weeks later the weather turned unusually warm for late November, so I opened the window next to my bed. And as I lay reading, a little goldfinch flew through the window and straight up twenty feet to perch on a steel support beam. After a few minutes, unable to find its way out, the bird panicked and started flying back and forth, swooping low over the heads of prisoners standing around or sitting on their bunks.

Oblivious to the little bird's plight, most prisoners laughed and pointed and ducked whenever the little bird dive-bombed them, but not Jack, who was clearly upset. As fast as his wheelchair allowed, he made his way over to my bed. "One of my birds got in here," he said, pointing up at the little bird now resting on a steel beam high above us.

"I know, Jack. I saw 'im when he flew through the window a few minutes ago."

"Why didn't ya stop 'im!"

"Jack, how was I gonna' stop 'im! That bird flew through the window so fast I couldn't do nothin'."

"What we gonna' do now," said Jack.? "We gotta get 'im outta here 'fore he flies into somethin' and bust his brains out."

"Ain't much we can do right now. When it gets dark and they turn out the lights, he'll settle down. And in the mornin' when it warms up a little, we'll open all the windows and the door, and he'll find his way out just like he found his way in. How's that sound?"

"What if he don't"

"Oh, he will, I guarantee ya. Bird's got good eyesight, better than we got. He'll see the light and fly outta here."

The next morning before daylight, Jack awakened me. "What is it, Jack?" I asked, propping up on one arm to look at my watch. "It's three-thirty in the mornin'."

"I been watchin' 'im," said Jack.

"Watchin' who, Jack? Who you talkin' about?"

"That little bird. I been watchin' 'im."

"You been up all night watchin' that bird!"

"Yeah, gotta' make sure weren't nobody messin' with 'im."

"Well, is he still up there? Is he alright?"

"I seen 'im up there on them pipes, eatin' bugs."

"Well, there's no shortage of bugs in here. I'm sure he's fat and happy. Truth be told, we oughta' invite about fifty of his bird friends to come help 'im. Maybe that'll help reduce the number of roaches we got."

"I think he likes it in here now."

"What he really likes is all them bugs, but still we need to get 'im outta here, so in a couple of hours, when it gets daylight and warms up, we'll get 'im out for sure."

"I don't see why we can't get 'im out right now."

"Because they ain't even turned the lights on yet, and everybody's still sleepin'. And it's cold outside. And you know well as I do that if we open all the windows, these dudes in here gonna get cold and start complainin'. Jack, the sun's not even up. It's still dark outside."

"It ain't that cold. Besides them sumbitches need to get up anyway," said Jack.

"You wouldn't say that if it was you. Just be patient and we'll get 'im out. Now, I'm goin' back to sleep for a couple more hours." I covered my eyes with a homemade sleeping mask and rolled over. Jack left.

Two hours later, just as the rising sun had begun to paint the green pine trees beyond the fences reddish-orange, I was awakened by a cold draft. Lifting my sleeping mask, I looked over to see that someone had opened the window by my bed. Just as I reached over to close the window, I heard a loud disturbance and turned to see Jack on the opposite side of the dormitory. He was sitting in his wheelchair parked near an open window. Surrounding him were a small group of men, pointing and yelling instructions to Hoghead, who was waving a long push broom overhead, trying to sweep the little bird off a steel support beam. As I watched, a few more men, awakened by the noise and the cold wind rushing through the windows, got up to join the melee. But most stayed in bed, wrapping themselves tightly in their blankets, cursing and threatening Jack and the rescue team.

Every time Hoghead swept at the goldfinch, the little bird simply hopped over the broom. Frustrated, Hoghead yelled, "You little bastard! I'll get ya!" Using the broom like a javelin, he threw it, hitting the bird a glancing blow. The bird fell. He landed on the concrete floor, motionless. All eyes turned toward Jack, and for a brief moment there was total silence.

"Then Jack broke the silence, yelling at Hoghead, "Ya kilt 'im, you sumbitch!".

"Well, hell Jack, I didn't mean to. He just kept jumpin' over the broom. I was just tryin' to get 'im off that beam up there, that's all," apologized Hoghead.

"You sumbitch. You sumbitch," muttered Jack, slowly pushing his wheelchair over to where the bird lay. He bent over and, with gnarled hands, picked up the limp body of the bird. He gently stroked it's tiny head with his forefinger, and amazingly, the little bird opened his eyes and looked up at Jack. "He come back," exclaimed Jack, wonder in his voice. He looked around at the faces of the men surrounding him. "He come back," he repeated.

Hoghead walked over. "I knew he weren't dead," he said. "Just stunned, that's all. I barely hit 'im with that broom."

Jack looked up at Hoghead. "You sumbitch," he said.

"Ah, come on, Jack, don't be sore. He's okay now."

Without another word, Jack, gently holding the bird, pumped his one foot on the floor and pushed his wheelchair across the dormitory to my bed.

"Is he okay?" I asked.

"Yep," said Jack, opening his cupped hands to show me the tiny bird. Jack then pushed his wheelchair close the wall and reached his hand out the window, giving the bird an opportunity to fly away. Instead, the goldfinch sat in the palm of Jack's open hand and looked up at him with eyes that shined like two tiny black beads. "Go on, little feller," encouraged Jack. "Go on. Get outta here." But the bird continued to sit in the palm of Jack's hand and stare up at him. Jack turned to me. "He don't wanna go," he said.

"Probably still stunned a little," I told him. "Why don't you try pushin' him off real easy with your other hand."

Jack gently raked the bird from his open hand. The bird fell below the open window and out of sight, and then, as if bouncing on a trampoline, he shot straight up.

"He's gone now," said Jack, turning to face me. I'm glad I got 'im outta here."

"Me too."

Less than a minute later, I said to Jack. "Don't start celebratin' yet."

"Huh?"

"Look behind you," I said. Jack turned to see the little bird sitting on the window ledge.

"I declare," said Jack, turning a joyous face in my direction. "If that don't beat all, he come back." Jack slowly reached out and the bird hopped onto the back of his hand.

"Now, I've seen it all," I said.

Jack flapped his arm up and down, trying to shake the bird off the back of his hand. "Go on," he said. "Get on outta here." But the bird hung on like a bronco rider. Again, Jack raked the bird off with his free hand, and this time the bird leapt into the air.

I joined Jack at the window and together we watched the goldfinch dip and dive a roller coaster path over the perimeter fences, then disappear into the woods a hundred yards distant. "He's gone for real this time," I said, putting my hand on Jack's shoulder.

Chapter Twenty-Five
The Ability to Daydream

Later that morning we sat on my bed drinking coffee and talking. "You know, Jack, it's really somethin' the way those birds took to you," I said.

"They knowed I'm tryin' to help 'em. Animals know that."

"Well, you're just a regular St. Francis, you know that."

"What?" Jack looked puzzled.

"St. Francis."

"Who's that?"

"He was one of them monks that lived a long time ago," I said. "I think they called him the patron saint of wildlife 'cause he protected birds and wild animals."

"Oh."

"I saw a paintin' of 'im on one of them little plastic cards the Catholics hand out. He was sittin' on a rock in the woods, surrounded by all kinds of birds and animals. There was even a little bird sittin' on his shoulder."

"But, I ain't no Catlick," said Jack. "Me and my mama went to the Church of God."

"Jack, I know you ain't Catholic. I was just sayin' you got the gift to tame birds and wild animals like that dude Saint Francis, that's all."

"Well, I ain't tried my hand at no wild animals yet."

"Well, who knows what the future holds," I joked.

"Humph," replied Jack. But he looked pleased.

"You know, Jack, I was just wonderin' - why do you think so many of these dudes in here wanted to help that little bird get free?"

"Hoghead nearly kilt 'im."

"Nah, He just got all worked up, that's all; he didn't mean to hurt 'im. But, you didn't' answer my question. Why do you think so many dudes wanted to help get that bird outta the dorm? Why'd you?"

"Ya' seen how scairt he was, flyin' around, nearly bumpin' into stuff. He didn't know where he was. Ain't no decent man in his right mind wants to see somethin' little like that, a little bird that ain't never hurt nobody, in a heap of trouble. Not when he knows he can help out."

"You got that right, Jack, and maybe since we can't get our own freedom, but at that moment had the power to give that little bird his, everybody jumped at the chance. It's like for once in our lives, we, all of us that tried to help, had the keys to this prison and could open the gate, maybe not for ourselves, but at least for that little bird."

"Did ya see how fast he flew over them fences? That was surely somethin', huh."

"Yeah, I saw 'im, Jack. That bird's probably halfway to Birmingham by now."

"That's a smart bird," said Jack, wistfully. "That's where I'd go if I could fly."

"Well, I think I'd just keep goin' and head further south. Maybe I wouldn't stop until I got all the way to the Florida Keys. Did you know that Key West is the farthest south you can go in the United States?" Jack didn't answer. I continued. "They got a big concrete marker in the middle of the street that says Key West: Southern Most Point in the USA or somethin' like that. I know, 'cause I've seen it. Did I tell you that I used to live in the Florida Keys?"

Again Jack didn't respond. Instead he just sat on the foot locker beside my bed staring into space, a melancholy look in his tired old eyes. I continued to daydream: "Man, Jack, it was so beautiful down there, makes me feel all big inside just thinkin' about it. All year 'round the water's warm, like bathtub water, and so clear you can see the fish swimmin' around in it. It's like you can just reach out and grab 'em. And the sand on the beaches, Jack - it's like that powdered sugar they put on them donuts they sell in the French Market in New Orleans. What do they call 'em? Oh yeah, beignets. And the Florida Keys got coconut trees everywhere. Hell, a man can live off the land down there if he's a mind to - just climb a coconut tree, get you a coconut, eat the meat, drink the milk. Wade out into the water and grab you a fish. Cook it right there on the beach. Man, what a life! Jack, if I could fly like that little bird, that's where I'd go."

"I'd just go home," said Jack.

The weather warmed and the goldfinches moved on. For weeks, every evening after supper, Jack asked me to push him onto the recreation yard, as close to the perimeter fences as allowed. There, he would sit until dusk, smoking his hand-rolled cigarettes and staring at the woods beyond the fences, trying to recapture what had been lost since childhood—the ability to daydream, the greatest gift a prisoner can give himself. But unlike me, Jack didn't dream of exotic locales; his fantasy was much simpler. He saw himself tucked safely inside his little clapboard house in the quiet neighborhood where he grew up. Nearby was his mother, and out back his work shed, packed full of junk to sort.

Chapter Twenty-Six
The Cinnamon Roll Caper

"You seen Caveman?" asked Rooster, standing at the foot of my bunk.

"I think he's in the TV area watchin' the news," I said.

"Good. I need to bend his ear," he said over his shoulder, hurrying away.

Rooster found Caveman sitting on one of the wooden benches in the TV area and sat down beside him. "What's up?" asked Rooster.

"Not much," said Caveman. "Just catchin' up on the news. What's up with you?"

"I was just thinkin'," said Rooster. "You know them cinnamon rolls you make are damn good."

"Everybody likes 'em. Me too. I probably eat about ten everytime I make 'em, especially when they just come outta the oven and are still hot."

"How about you make a few dozen extra next time you make 'em and I sell 'em for 'ya. I know I can get a dollar a piece for "em, especially if you make 'em big and fat with lots of icin'. We could split the profit."

"That sounds good. Only one problem," said Caveman. "How we gonna get 'em outta the kitchen. You know they shake me down every time my shift's over. Won't let me bring nothin' out. I can eat all I want while I'm workin', but they won't let me take nothin' outta the kitchen."

"Hey, no problem," said Rooster. "I think I know a way to get 'em out. You game?"

"Hell yeah, if you can get 'em out," said Caveman. "How many cinnamon rolls we talkin' about?"

"I don't know. Maybe three or four dozen to start. Let's see how it goes."

"Well, look," said Caveman. "I bake cinnamon rolls every Tuesday for supper. I can get away with making four dozen extra—I'll put 'em up somewhere. Now tell me, how we're gonna get 'em outta the kitchen?"

"This is what I want you to do," said Rooster. "Take the cinnamon rolls and wrap 'em up in some of that plastic wrap. Wrap 'em up real good; make sure they're waterproof, then take 'em and put 'em in a clean trash bag. Tie it up tight. Hide the bag somewhere until after you clean up, then put the bag of cinnamon rolls in the bottom of a clean plastic trash barrel. Cover the bag with a flat piece of cardboard, then just fill the barrel with a full bag of trash. When I bring the cart up after supper to get the barrels, I'll dig out the bag with the cinnamon rolls in it, give em' to Hoghead to take back to the dorm, then we'll sell 'em and split the money with you. How's that sound?"

"Sounds good, but how you gonna know which trash barrel's got the cinnamon rolls in it? I mean, after supper we probably got five or six barrels of trash?"

"Easy," said Rooster. "Use this." He handed Caveman a red magic marker. "Mark the trash barrel with the cinnamon rolls in it with this magic marker. Just put a big X on it. The guard won't think nothin' about it. But just mark that one barrel."

"Alright," said Caveman. "I'll give it a try. Today's Friday. I'll make em' Tuesday."

"Deal," said Rooster. He fist-bumped Caveman, then walked off.

Next Tuesday after supper, Rooster, followed by Hoghead pushing a mop and mop bucket, pushed the trash cart to the loading dock in back of the kitchen. Sitting on the dock were five barrels of trash. "There they are," Rooster told Hoghead. "Now when I find the cinnamon rolls, you put 'em in the mop bucket and take em' on back to the dorm while I empty the rest of these barrels and rinse em' out."

"I thought you said the barrel with the cinnamon rolls in it had a red X marked on it. I don't see none of 'em marked," said Hoghead.

Rooster walked over and spun each barrel until he found one with a crude X drawn on it. "Here it is," said Rooster. "It was just facin' the other way." He dug into the barrel, pulled out the full trash bag and threw it to the side. He then removed a piece of cardboard to find the trash bag with the cinnamon rolls. He dumped the bag into Hoghead's mop bucket. "See you back at the house," said Rooster.

Hoghead hurried away, carefully pushing the mop bucket full of precious cargo down the blacktop in the direction of the dorm, while Rooster cleaned the rest of the trash barrels.

A couple hours later Rooster walked into the dormitory to find Hoghead sitting on his bunk eating a cinnamon roll and drinking a cup of coffee. "Hey, you ain't eatin' up all our profit, are you?"

"Hell no," said Hoghead. "I figured I deserved at least one, all the hustlin' I been doin'." Before Rooster could respond, Hoghead said, "Man, I done sold almost two dozen cinnamon rolls. Look!" He took a final bite, rubbed his hands on his pants, and opened the footlocker beside his bed. The locker was stuffed with Ramen noodles, candy bars and chips. "And that ain't countin' the ones I sold on credit 'til store day."

"Hope you didn't sell too many on credit," said Rooster. "I don't feel like chasin' these dudes down to get my money come store day."

"Nah," said Hoghead. "Just a couple, and to dudes I know gonna pay. Besides, after what you did to Charley and Patch, doubt anybody's gonna try to stiff ya'"

"Never know. Some of these dudes is just fuckin' ignorant; they don't believe shit stinks. But I'll tell you what, if they don't pay when they're supposed to, then I'm gonna charge em' interest every week til' they do."

"Hell, it's just a coupla dollars," said Hoghead.

"I don't care if it's a penny. They owe, they gotta pay, and they don't pay on time, I'm chargin' 'em interest."

"Alright, I'll tell em'."

Chapter Twenty-Seven
Crab Nature

The cinnamon roll caper worked well for a few months and Rooster, Hoghead and Caveman prospered, especially Rooster, who extended credit and charged interest to those few who were slow to pay. But more importantly, he saved most of what he earned from the sale of the cinnamon rolls and opened a store, charging an exorbitant hundred per cent interest. For example, if a fellow prisoner borrowed two noodles, he had to agree to repay four noodles back at an agreed upon date, usually the next store day, and if he failed to pay on time, he was charged interest. Two dollars in store goods could easily cost a prisoner in arrears four dollars, six dollars, eight dollars, or more. In addition, Rooster loaned store goods to a few prisoners for cash deposited in his prison account. He then used the cash to buy more goods from the prison store to boost his inventory.

One of the prisoners who worked on the baking crew in the kitchen with Caveman noticed that he seemed to be prospering: Caveman wore new tennis shoes, was smoking packaged cigarettes, and had a full locker box. Curious, he watched Caveman closely and soon discovered the secret to his sudden prosperity. Then the prisoner did something quite petty. He waited until after Caveman had wrapped the freshly baked cinnamon rolls in a clean trash bag and had put the bag in the trash barrel, then (when no one was looking) stole the bag of cinnamon rolls and hid them under a box of celery in one of the freezers.

Later that day when Rooster and Hoghead searched the marked trash barrel and then the other barrels as well, and found nothing, they left, frustrated and befuddled.

That evening Rooster walked in the dormitory. I was lying on my bed reading. On the bunk next to mine Caveman was napping. "Hey, wake up." Rooster shook him awake.

Caveman opened his eyes, looked up at Rooster. "Yeah, what's up?" he asked.

"What happened this week? You couldn't make the cinnamon rolls?"

"What're you talkin' about?" said Caveman, sitting up. "I made em'. Four dozen. Put em' in the trash barrel like I always do."

"Well, I looked through the barrel. Matter of fact, I looked through all the barrels, and no cinnamon rolls."

"Damn! Son-of-a-bitch!" shouted Caveman. "Some bastard musta seen me and stoled em'. "

I put my book down. "Sure, you checked all the barrels?" I asked.

"Yeah, I checked em'. Even had Hoghead check em'. No cinnamon rolls,"said Rooster. He turned to Caveman. "Who you think got em'?"

"I don't know. Might be that dude that cleans up, or probably somebody works on the bakery crew with me. Them some lowdown dudes, anyway. Hate to see a dude come up. Always trying to pull somebody down when they see 'im doin' good. But one thing's for sure though, they can't sell 'em, 'cause then we'll know who stoled 'em."

"Got that right," said Rooster. "They can't sell 'em and ain't nobody can eat four dozen cinnamon rolls, so what are they gonna do with 'em?"

"Probably eat a few, then, outta spite throw the rest away," said Caveman.

"That don't make no sense," said Rooster.

"It's like crabs in a bucket," I interjected.

"Crabs in a bucket? What you talkin' about?" asked Caveman.

"Well, when I was a kid I used to go crabbin', you know - tie a chicken neck to a string, throw it in the water, wait for a crab to start feedin' on it, then slowly pull it in, then grab the crab with a net on a long pole."

"I used to do that in Mobile, in the bay, just off the Causeway," said Rooster.

"Then I'd put the crabs in a bucket," I continued. "But, there was always one or two crabs that would try to crawl up the side of the bucket to get out."

"Can't blame em'," said Caveman. "If I was a crab in a bucket, I'd try to get out too. But what's that got to do with somebody stealin' the cinnamon rolls?"

"It ain't got nothin' to do with cinnamon rolls, but it's got a lot to do with crab nature. You see, there's always this one crab crawlin' up the inside of the bucket, just about to the top, almost out, when one of the crabs in the bucket with 'im will grab his fin or leg or whatever and pull him back down into the bucket. Then another crab will try to get out and another one will pull 'im back down too, over and over. You're right - ain't got nothin' to do with cinnamon rolls, but when you said how some dudes in here hate to see somebody come up, that reminded me of crabs in a bucket. So, I guess it ain't just crab nature, but it's human nature too."

"Well, I guess we're gonna have to figure out another way to get em' out," said Caveman.

"Guess so," said Rooster. "Let me think about it. Meanwhile, you hear of somebody sellin' cinnamon rolls, let me know."

"I doubt anybody's stupid enough to do that," said Caveman.

"Maybe it's best you don't know," I said.

"Why's that?" asked Rooster.

"'Cause if you don't know, then you won't feel obligated to do somethin' you'll regret—somethin' that will just land you back in the doghouse . . . or worse. If I was you, I wouldn't even worry about it," I said. "Cut your losses. You've made enough off the cinnamon rolls to set yourself up in a store. You don't need to hustle cinnamon rolls no more."

"Yeah, you're right," said Rooster. "But it's the principle of the thing that gets me. I just hope nobody don't start sellin' cinnamon rolls. 'Cause if they do I'll have no choice, I'll have to do somethin'."

"Let's hope," I said.

Chapter Twenty-Eight
Kicked Out In the Cold

It was a cold, rainy morning. Rooster and I were sitting in the TV area watching the news when we heard a loud argument at the other end of the dormitory. "What the hell's all that racket?" Rooster asked. We looked at each other, then both turned to see Jack, naked except for a pair of boxer shorts and a white, knit cap, sitting in his wheelchair beside his bed. He was yelling at a tall, muscular guard holding a clipboard. "I told you, you sumbitch, I done had that test!"

The guard stood over Jack. "Don't gimme no shit, you old bastard!" He jabbed the clipboard with his finger. "It says right here, you're on list for a blood test this mornin', and you're goin'!"

"Oh shit," said Rooster. "Looks like Jack's at it again."

"Damn," I said.

"I ain't goin'!" yelled Jack.

"Oh, you're goin'!" shouted the guard. "Even if I have to drag your sorry old ass up there myself!"

"Let's go check it out and see what the problem is," I said.

"The problem's Jack," said Rooster. "It's always Jack."

We reached Jack's bed just in time to hear the old man yell, "I ain't goin'! I done had my blood took!"

I knew that Jack was telling the truth because earlier that morning I had pushed him to the infirmary for the blood test, but I didn't intervene, hoping that the guard would finally just let it go. Unfortunately, he was as stubborn as Jack. "Oh, we'll see about that!" said the guard. He grabbed the handles of Jack's wheelchair and spun it around.

"Let go, you sumbitch! Let go!" screamed Jack, his eyes wild, slobber dripping onto his unshaven chin. When the guard attempted to push the chair, Jack stretched out his one leg and planted his foot to try to stop the forward movement of the chair, but the guard was too strong, and the chair continued to move toward the front door. Rooster and I followed.

"I told you, you of son of a bitch, you're goin' to the infirmary!" yelled the guard, forcing the wheelchair closer to the front door.

I stepped in front of the wheelchair and the guard paused, glaring at me. "What the fuck you want!" he yelled.

"Look," I said calmly. "He's tellin' you the truth. I pushed 'im up to the infirmary myself early this mornin' for his insulin and that blood test. If you don't believe me, all you gotta do is call up there and check."

"I ain't callin' nobody. Now, you better get your ass out of the way and go sit down somewhere! This ain't none of your business!"

Using all the self-control I could muster, I backed away. Followed by Rooster, I walked over to my bed and we both sat on it. "Look, don't sweat it," said Rooster. "That bastard's just ignorant. Needs to learn how to talk to people."

"All he's gotta do is make a phone call. Call up there and they'll tell 'im Jack's already had that blood test. I don't understand it."

"Him doin' that would be too much like right," said Rooster. "If he called up there then he'd have to admit that he made a mistake, and he ain't gonna do that. No way."

Sitting there, we watched the guard reach over the top of Jack's wheelchair and push open the heavy, steel door. A blast of freezing rain rushed in, chilling us where we sat not ten foot away. The guard then grabbed the handles of Jack's wheelchair and tried to force the chair through the open door, but Jack reached out and grabbed the doorframe with both hands, stopping the chair from passing through. Finally, the guard let go of the wheelchair's handles, stepped back and viciously kicked the wheelchair through the doorway. Jack's wheelchair shot down the concrete ramp out front, spun in a half-circle, teetered on one wheel, and then in slow motion, slid off the ramp and fell two feet, dumping Jack onto the wet, frozen blacktop.

The guard slammed the door shut, turned and announced to everyone watching: "I'm the one runs this dorm, you hear! And when I tell one of you convicts to do somethin', you best do it pronto . . .

or else you're gonna get your ass handed to you! Got that!" Nobody responded.

I grabbed my blanket off my bed, and Rooster and I headed toward the door. There we were met by the guard. "Where the hell you two goin'?" he asked.

"You didn't have to do that," I said.

"Yeah, that old man's almost seventy-five," said Rooster.

"I don't give a fuck he's a hundred seventy- five," said the guard. "He's gonna learn that if I tell him he's a duck, he better start quackin'."

I struggled to stay calm. "Hey, I understand you're runnin' things around here, but it's freezin' cold and rainin' out there, and that old man's almost naked," I said. "All you had to do was call up to the infirmary and they woulda told you he's already had his blood test this mornin'."

"Look, I already told you I ain't gotta call nobody, and anyway, that old bastard's got a smart mouth on 'im. And I done told both of you twice to go sit down and mind your own business!"

"Jack is my business. He's my friend," I stepped around the guard and continued toward the door. Rooster followed.

"If ya'll go out there and help that old bastard, I'll have both your asses locked up in the doghouse!" shouted the guard.

"Well then, that's your business," I said. "Besides, it won't be my first time in the doghouse."

"Me neither," said Rooster. "I just got out and I don't give a fuck whether I go back or not."

We walked past the guard and out the door to find Jack sitting on the wet asphalt beside his overturned wheelchair. In his hand he held his wet knit cap. He was staring at it, a stunned look on his face. Jack's skin had turned blue, and blood trickled down the side of his face from a gash on his forehead.

"You okay, Jack?" I asked, righting Jack's wheelchair.

"My new hat got wet," said Jack.

"Don't worry 'bout the hat," I said. "It'll dry out. But it looks like you got a pretty nasty cut on your forehead."

Jack rubbed his forehead, looked at his bloody hand, then wiped his hand on his boxer shorts.

"Here, let me help you into your chair," I said, grabbing Jack under the arms and lifting him into his wheelchair. I covered him with the blanket. "That cut on your head might need some stitches. Want me to go ahead and push you up to the infirmary so they can look at it?"

"I ain't goin' to the infirmary!" protested Jack. "I done said I ain't goin', and I ain't goin'!"

"Okay, okay. I understand. Have it your way. How 'bout I just push you back inside and get you outta this weather?"

While Rooster held the door, I pushed Jack's chair back up the ramp and inside the dormitory. Just inside, Rooster asked, "You got this?"

"Yeah," I said. "I'll just push him over to his bed."

"Well, look, I'll holler at you later, I gotta go pick up the trash," said Rooster. He mumbled, "Look, I told you - don't let Jack get you into somethin' you can't get out of."

"I remember, but come on, just look what that guard done to 'im. Am I supposed to just sit by and let Jack get abused by that bastard?"

"I understand, but sometimes you gotta know when to butt out."

"Gotcha," I said. "Well, it's over now. I'll holler at you later." I turned to Jack. "Want me to push you over to the sink so you can wash that blood off?"

"I can do it myself," snapped Jack.

"Okay, okay," I said, throwing up my hands. "You're on your own."

Using his one leg, Jack slowly pushed his wheelchair, not to the toilet area or to his bed, but over to the TV area where the guard now sat watching TV. He stopped directly behind the guard and said, "Told you, you sumbitch, I wasn't goin' to no damn infirmary."

The guard turned, then stood to face Jack. "I've had it up to here with you, you old bastard! Now go lay down on your bed before I really get at your old ass!"

When Jack didn't move, the guard stood, pulled his wooden baton and stepped closer.

Watching from my bed, I said out loud, "Oh shit!" then rushed over to stand between Jack and the guard. "Now, hold it just a minute," I said, holding up open hands. "You don't wanna'. . ."

Pain shot throughout my entire body, paralyzing my left arm, as the guard cracked me across the left shoulder with his baton. I grabbed my shoulder with my right hand and bent over, grimacing. Then, using the stick like a goad, the guard rammed the baton into my solar plexus. I crumbled to the floor, gasping for breath.

Jack grabbed the arms of his wheelchair and tried to push himself up so that he could help me, but when the guard saw him trying to stand, he whacked Jack on both hands. Jack howled in pain and sank back into his chair. The guard rushed in and pushed the tip of his wooden baton into the hollow of Jack's neck, pinning him to the seat of his wheelchair. "Don't you dare fuckin' move," said the guard, "or I'll break your neck." The guard keyed his radio and announced, "Code Blue! I repeat, Code Blue!"

Within minutes, several guards rushed into the dormitory. Jack and I were both hand- cuffed and taken to the infirmary. The gash on Jack's head was treated and he was released back into population. The nurse examined my shoulder and gave me some muscle rub and ibuprofen. Then I was taken to the doghouse and later charged and found guilty of

DOC
CONVICT

interfering with an officer during the course of his
duty. I was sentenced to spend the next thirty days
in the doghouse.

Even worse, I lost my job in the library.

Chapter Twenty-Nine
Déjà Vu

Pacing the cell, I stopped at every turn to massage my left shoulder. Of course it's my left side, I thought. It's always the left side. Then I realized that twenty years earlier I would have seen the unfortunate incident with Jack and the guard, my present injury, and my current internment in the doghouse, as no big deal - nothing more than a consequence of doing time. Now, however, I found it disturbing and worrisome. I thought I had learned a little more self-control than that, I told myself. But what could I have done differently? I guess the big mistake I made was stepping in between Jack and the guard. Rooster was right. Sometimes, you gotta know when to mind your own business. I sighed. Nah, to hell with that! Sometimes you just gotta stand up, even if you get whacked in the process.

I sat down on the concrete bed, reached over and picked up a stiff, dark blue blanket that reeked of urine and body odor. Folding it to make a pillow, I lay down, and in that liminal space between wakefulness and sleep, I thought about my childhood. I tried to remember just one pleasant experience, but couldn't. There has to be one, I thought. Yeah, my childhood was miserable but there has to be at least one pleasant experience, probably several. Yet I can't recall even one. It's as if there are so many unpleasant childhood memories

that they've taken up all the available space in my
head, crowding out any pleasant ones that may be
there.

All I could remember of my childhood was a blur
of drunken fights between my parents, their verbal
and physical abuse, the many days when there was
little or no food to eat, the evictions, moving from
house to house and state to state, and the suffering
and embarrassment of poverty and abuse.

I've made so many mistakes in my life; so many. I
wish I could turn back time and do it all over again.
But what would be the point? Hell, even if I could,
I wouldn't remember what little life has taught me
so far. Surely, I'd make the same mistakes or even
worse, and find myself in a worse predicament. I
looked around the cell. It didn't seem it could be
any worse, but I knew it could always be worse; that
much I had learned.

I tried to sleep but couldn't, so I finally gave up.
I paced the cell while continuing to massage my
shoulder. When I tired of pacing, I lay back down
and stared at the ceiling ten feet above me.

Despite the monotony, the thirty days passed
quickly. My shoulder healed, even if my spirit didn't
completely. I was released from the doghouse and
sent back to the same dormitory. I wasn't surprised
when I saw that the same officer who had attacked
me and Jack was still working there. I felt uneasy
and vowed to avoid him whenever possible.

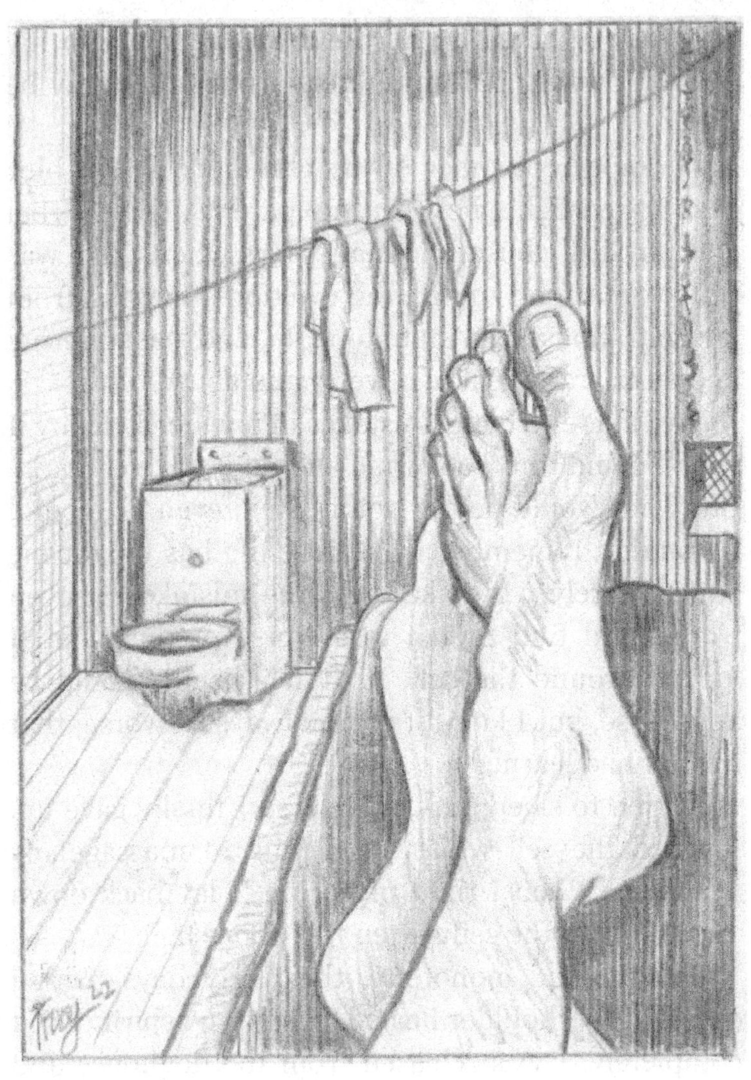

I had just finished stowing my personal property and making my bed when Rooster and Caveman showed up. "Man, it's good to see you back," said Rooster.

"Did you get that extra chicken tray I sent ya?" asked Caveman.

"What extra tray? I didn't get no extra chicken tray," I said.

"Damn, can't trust nobody to do nothin' here at Donaldson," said Caveman. "I sent an extra chicken tray with that kitchen guy takes the trays to the doghouse. He was supposed to give it to ya."

"Well, I didn't get it. Musta got waylaid by somebody."

"Shit," said Caveman. "I'll find out what happened to it."

"Don't matter now, I'm outta there. Anybody seen Jack around?"

"Well, I got some bad news for ya," said Rooster.

"That's just what I need, bad news. What is it?"

"Jack's dead."

"Aw, man, you gotta be kiddin'. How'd he die? "

"Well, after you went to the doghouse, Jack got real sick and caught pneumonia. It got so bad they had to send him outside to the free world hospital again. And I heard from this dude works in the infirmary he died a couple weeks later."

I turned to look at the officer sitting in a chair at the other end of the dormitory and said, "That bastard. It's all his fault. He's the one caused it, kickin' Jack out into the cold like that."

"Don't worry, he'll get his sooner or later. They always do," said Caveman. "Just wait and see."

Four days later, Rooster rushed into the dormitory and interrupted me on my bed reading. "You ain't gonna believe what I got to tell ya," he said.

"Try me. Ain't nothin' surprises me no more here at Donaldson."

"This will!" Rooster paused. "I just seen 'em wheelin' Jack in the back gate. Jack's alive!"

"What!" I stood up. "You gotta' be shittin' me. right."

"I'm serious," said Rooster. "I just saw him at the back gate. They took him up to the infirmary."

"You just told me a couple days ago that he was dead."

"That's what I heard, too. But believe me, he's alive, 'cause I just seen him with my own eyes. I even offered to push his wheelchair, but they wouldn't let me. Jack saw me though. He waved."

That evening, I walked up to the infirmary to ask if I could talk to Jack, but the guard in the control center refused to let me. I left, planning to try again tomorrow.

The next morning, again Rooster, along with Hoghead, rushed into the dormitory and straight to my bed. Caveman had just come in from work in the kitchen and we were sitting on my bunk drinking coffee and talking. This time Rooster didn't beat around the bush. "Jack's dead," he said. But before I could respond, Rooster continued: "Early this mornin', I went up to the infirmary to pick the trash and heard he died at breakfast."

"Rooster, what the fuck you talkin' about! You just told me yesterday you saw him alive!"

"He was alive yesterday, but he died this mornin'."

"You sure this time?"

"Swear to God," said Rooster. "He's dead for sure this time. Saw the body myself. They had him zipped up in one of them body bags layin' on a table."

"Sure it was Jack in the bag?" asked Caveman.

"That's the same thing I asked the nurse," said Rooster. "She told me it was him."

"How'd he die? Was it the pneumonia that got 'im?" I asked.

"Nah. It's the damdest thing you ever heard," said Rooster. He then told me and Hoghead and Caveman how Jack had died.

"Damn!", I said. "After all those close calls! Imagine 'im dyin' like that."

"I ain't never heard of nobody dying like that, not in prison, anyway. That's some strange shit," said Hoghead.

"Me neither," said Rooster, "but the nurse told me she's seen a lot of old people die like that. Still, I'm with you, Hoghead, that's some strange shit." Rooster looked out the window. The sky was overcast and a light rain fell. "I see an ambulance at the back gate," he said. "It's probably the county morgue come to pick up Jack's body."

"Let's go see," I said.

"Shit, it's rainin' out there," said Hoghead.

"It's just barely sprinklin'," I said.

"Come on, Hoghead, I know you're sweet as sugar, but you ain't gonna melt." Rooster laughed.

"Fuck you," said Hoghead.

Chapter Thirty
Eulogy

Behind a ten-foot fence topped with razor wire, the four prisoners stood in the light rain and watched the ambulance drive through the back gate and park under a tall gun tower. Two medical attendants got out. The gate slid open. Followed by a guard, they pushed a gurney past.

Hunching his shoulders and wiping his head, Hoghead said, "Ya ever notice how in the movies it's always rainin' at a funeral."

"That's just a gimmick they use in Hollywood to set the mood," said Rooster. "Besides, this ain't no funeral. They just comin' to pick up Jack's body."

"I guess it's true this time," I said. "Jack's really dead."

"Yep, he's gone this time, but you gotta' give it to Jack, he was a tough old buzzard," said Hoghead.

"Tough as they come," said Rooster. "To tell you the truth, I was beginnin' to think nothin' could kill 'im."

"He came close to death a coupla times, that's for sure," said Caveman, "but he always pulled through."

"Well, not this time," said Hoghead.

"Nope, not this time," said Rooster, turning to me. "How long you think before they cart his body out?"

"I don't know," I said. "Maybe twenty or thirty minutes, but however long it takes I'm gonna stay right here 'til they bring 'im out. I wanna kinda pay my last respects. Feel like I owe Jack that much."

"Well, I don't feel like I owe im' nothin," said Caveman. "I mean, let's face it, he wasn't all that respectful himself, but then I didn't know 'im like you dudes did. Still, I'll hang with ya 'cause I got respect for you guys."

"I'll stay 'til they bring 'im out," said Rooster.

"I'll hang with you too," said Hoghead. "Told you I knew Jack on the streets. Even knew his old man before he died." Hoghead chuckled. "You think Jack was hard to get along with, shoulda met his old man. He was somethin' else."

"Yeah, you told me that," I said. "And I know Jack was hard to get along with at times, but like my grandpa used to say, he had gumption. And he never gave up, no matter what life threw at 'im, and life threw a lot at 'im. Gotta' admire that."

"That's true," said Rooster, "but it's also true that Jack couldn't never admit when he was wrong neither."

"That's true for most people, especially here," said Caveman.

"And Jack was always negative and super paranoid," said Rooster. "You gotta admit that, too."

"I know. I know," I said. "And he was angry and selfish and all that, but Rooster, I swear, even with all that, just hangin' out with Jack somehow made me feel better about myself and I can't explain why."

"I can," said Caveman.

"How's that?"

"Well," said Caveman, "it's kinda like Jack was the perfect example of how people ain't supposed to act. And hangin' out with him was bound to make anybody look good. Know what I mean."

"Well, you might be right," I said. "Maybe I did hang out with 'im just to make myself look good, but I think there was more to it than that. I kinda felt like I was lookin' out for 'im, and the truth is . . . helpin' Jack made me just feel good, and maybe too, I was hopin' that when I get old like Jack somebody'll look out for me."

"Kinda like what them smart folks call karma," said Rooster. "You know, like one good turn deserves another."

"Well, not exactly," I said, "but something like that."

"That might be what all 'em smart folks say," said Caveman "but let me tell ya things in life don't always turn out fair. Not everybody gets what they deserve, and others get more than they deserve. No, life ain't always fair. That much I know for sure."

The wind picked up, and I looked past Rooster to see a bank of storm clouds in the distance. "I know it seems that way," I said, "but I really do believe everything kinda balances out in the end."

"You know, I don't think Jack had nobody left on the streets," interrupted Hoghead. "What ya think they'll do with his body?"

"Probably bury 'im in what they call a pauper's grave," I said. "I heard that sometimes they do that when convicts die and they ain't got no family to pick up the body. I also heard that sometimes they donate the body to medical schools, just to give them student doctors somethin' to practice on. That's what I read anyway."

"Yeah, I heard about that too, and I don't want nobody cuttin' on me when I'm dead," said Hoghead, "carvin' me up like a Thanksgivin' turkey just to see what makes me tick."

"Hell, Hoghead, what difference does it make. You'll be dead, you ain't gonna' feel nothin' anyway," said Rooster.

"Maybe so," said Hoghead, "but ain't nobody knows for sure."

"You're right, ain't nobody knows for sure what happens after ya die," said Caveman. "Still, if they wanna cut me up, and it'll help some doctor learn, I say, have at it."

"I growed up believin' that when we die we go to heaven or hell, and it all depends on how we been livin' our lives. And I know I'll probably go to hell, but I want to go just like God made me, not in little pieces," said Hoghead.

"Well, I ain't disagreein', but I've read that some people feel different about what happens after we die," I said.

"How's that?" asked Rooster.

"Some people believe heaven or hell ain't someplace you go to after you die, but it's right here on earth. And that every moment, dependin' on what we think or do, we create our own heaven or hell."

"You sure come up with some strange shit sometimes. Ya gotta quit readin' all them weird books," said Hoghead. "They're fuckin' up your head."

"Ain't strange, just different. Besides, that ain't somethin' I come up with. Billions of people believe that, and some even believe in what they call reincarnation - that we come back again after we die, maybe over and over."

"I'm gonna' just stick to what the Bible says," said Hoghead. "I believe it's good for a man to have somethin' to believe in . . . somethin' that gives him hope, and what it says in the Bible gives me hope."

"And I'm gonna' keep believin' that when you die, that's it . . . lights out. When you're dead, you're dead," said Rooster. "You ain't goin' to no heaven or hell and you ain't gonna keep comin' back over and over."

"Well, like Caveman said, ain't nobody knows for sure what happens to us after we die, but I do know one thing for sure," I said.

"What's that?" asked Caveman.

"There's one thing for sure that survives us after we're dead, it's memories."

"How we gonna' have memories if we're dead?" asked Rooster. "We ain't gonna remember nothin'. We're just dead."

"I ain't talkin' about our memories, I'm talkin' about the memories that other people have about us," I said. "I'm talkin' about the memories of people that's still alive. . . what they remember most about us after we die. We got to ask ourself, will they have good memories or bad memories about us? 'Cause that'll be part of what they call our legacy."

"Our what?" asked Caveman.

"Our legacy," I said. "You know, what we leave behind. I mean we ain't got no money or prestige, ain't accomplished nothin' important, so all we got to leave behind is the memories we leave in the minds of those that knew us. What they remember most about us will be our legacy."

"If I don't give a damn what people think about me while I'm alive, and I damn sure ain't gonna care what they think about me after I'm dead," said Rooster.

"I'd like to think that after I'm gone, people won't remember all the bad shit I done," said Caveman, "but just some of the good things."

"That's just how I'm gonna' remember Jack," I told Caveman. "I'm not gonna think about all the petty or bad things he did, but I'm gonna remember the good things he did."

"Like what?" said Rooster. "Name just one."

"Well, like how he tried to save that little bird, for one thing. I know you remember that. And how Jack had a certain integrity, even if he was hard to get along with at times."

"Integrity! What integrity? You sayin' Jack was honest?" asked Rooster.

"Yeah, more than most in here. I know he didn't have much, but if he owed somebody, he always tried to pay best way he could. That can't be said about a lot of dudes in here. And he told the truth, how he saw it anyway, no matter the consequences, which in here ain't always a good thing, but it's an honest thing."

"You're right about that. Speakin' your mind in prison is a quick way to get your ass handed to ya," said Rooster. "Matter of fact, it ain't always good to speak your mind anywhere, in prison or out."

"Rooster's right," said Caveman. "You know what one of the most dangerous weapons in the world is?"

"Probably one of them nuclear weapons," said Hoghead.

"No," said Caveman. "It's the mouth, especially in prison. I can't tell you the number of dudes I've seen get fucked up in prison because of their mouths. Yes sir, the mouth is one of the most dangerous weapons there is."

"I can't argue with that," I said. "No doubt Jack had a big problem with his mouth. I guess you could say that it was speaking his mind finally got him killed. All he had to do was shut up arguing with that guard, and act like he was going to the infirmary. Hell, he didn't even have to go up there. All he had to do was act like he was going up there, and then that guard wouldn't have kicked him outside naked in the cold, then he wouldn't caught pneumonia, got sent to the hospital, then the infirmary where he died. But that just wasn't Jack's nature, and so he paid the price. But you know what might be almost as bad as being remembered mostly for the bad things we did after we die?"

"What?" asked Caveman.

"Not being remembered at all. Being born, livin' your life, and then dyin' unnoticed, as if you never existed at all."

"Well, ain't that what happens to most people," said Rooster. "We can't all be famous like Elvis. Most of us just ordinary people, livin' ordinary lives."

"That's true, and maybe the four of us might not be remembered at all after we're dead, but I've made up my mind - I ain't gonna let that happen to Jack. Look, I know that old man wasn't nothin' special, but his life was important to me. And I tell you what. I kinda been teachin' myself how to write the last few years."

"I see you readin' all the time, but I didn't know you was tryin' to learn how to write too," said Hoghead.

"Might as well, I got plenty of time on my hands."

"You ain't the only one," said Caveman.

"And one day, I'm gonna write about Jack. Hell, I might even put all ya'll in it. But mainly it's gonna be about Jack. I'm gonna let the world know that this ornery little man with the eyes of a child and the heart of a lion existed, and for a short time walked this earth."

"I'd like to be in a book," said Caveman. "Can you write in there that I was good-lookin'?"

"Damn, Caveman, he ain't gonna write no fantasy," said Rooster, laughing.

"Fuck you, Rooster," said Caveman. "You ain't exactly no movie star yourself."

"I might not be, but I sure as hell ain't no star in a monster movie like you."

"Damn, you aiming pretty high, ain't you?" asked Hoghead. "And even if you do write about Jack, what makes you think people gonna want to read about somebody like him, or even about us for that matter. And how you gonna get somebody to make it into a book?".

"All I can do is try," I said.

"Well, on second thought, Jack might make an interestin' story, especially the way he died. Now that weren't ordinary, that's for sure. No sir, nothin' ordinary about that," said Rooster.

"Tell me again how he died," said Caveman.

Chapter Thirty-One
Somethin' Between Me and Jack

"Well, this is what I heard happened. He died at breakfast time," said Rooster. "When they brought the breakfast trays, Jack wouldn't get up to eat, so they handed him his tray and he ate his breakfast layin' on his back with the tray sittin' on his stomach. They said he choked to death on a biscuit. Can you believe that! After all the close calls Jack had, they said Jack finally died by choking on a biscuit!"

"Didn't nobody try to help him . . . call for the nurse or somethin'?" asked Caveman.

"Well, I heard there was this other dude up there in the infirmary with him. But he didn't try to do nothin' to help. They said the dude just sat there eatin' his own breakfast and watching cartoons on TV while Jack choked to death. And even after Jack died, he didn't call for the nurse. They didn't discover Jack was dead until after the nurse came around to give him his insulin. She's the one that found him dead."

"Who was the son of a bitch in the ward with him?" I asked.

"You ain't gonna believe this," said Rooster.

"Try me," I said.

"It was that young dude, Jerry."

"You mean the same dude that Jack hit in the head with that cane of his?" said Hoghead.

"One and the same. He was up there just overnight waitin' to go to the free world hospital for a hernia operation," said Rooster.

"You don't think Jerry smothered him or somethin' do ya?" said Hoghead. "I heard Jerry tell Jack that he was gonna get him."

"Who knows," said Rooster. Rooster turned, stepped closer to the fence. "Look. They're bringin' Jack out right now."

We all stepped closer to the fence and watched as the two medical attendants, again escorted by a guard, pushed the gurney toward the back gate. On the gurney was Jack in a body bag covered with a wrinkled, purple shroud made of cheap velvet. When the gurney was directly in front of where we stood, so close that I could have reached out and touched him had the fence not been there, I grabbed the fence, leaned in and whispered, "Well this is it, old friend, the struggle's over now. You're finally free. I know you always thought I was smart, even if you didn't say so, but the truth is, Jack, I ain't really that smart - I just been locked up a long time and I've had plenty of time to read a lot of books, and I got a pretty good memory, so I remembered a lot. Still, there's so much I don't know. Like I'm not even sure if there is a heaven or a hell after we die. For all I know, heaven for you might just be as simple as you holdin' that little bird in your hands when it came back to life, and hell might be the pain you felt when you heard your mama died. And then, maybe heaven and hell is different for everybody. I don't know.

"But, Jack, all that said, I do believe there's a God or Higher Power or whatever you wanna call It somewhere, and I believe that He created all we see around us, and I believe He favors people like you, 'cause He knows that underneath that crusty front you was always puttin' on, your heart was good. And if there is a heaven out there somewhere, that's where you're goin', and for all eternity you'll be doin' what you loved most in life: diggin' through your junk; takin' care of your mama, and feedin' those little birds."

"What'd ya say?" asked Caveman.

"Nothin'" I replied. "Just somethin' between me and Jack." I let go of the fence, turned, wiped the rain out of my eyes, looked at Rooster, Hoghead, and Caveman. "Well, he's gone now," I said.

"Yeah, he's gone," said Hoghead. "Let's get outta this rain."

We left the recreation yard and walked toward the dorm.

"Looks like it's clearin' up now," said Caveman.

"Yeah, the sun's comin' out," said Rooster.

"That ain't all's comin' out," said Hoghead, pointing at the woods beyond the perimeter fences. "Look."

We all stopped, turned, and saw a flock of goldfinch circle the recreation yard, then land in the grassy area in front of 2 dorm. "I guess they're back for another Donaldson winter," I said.

"They're early this year," said Caveman.

"Maybe they come back early to pay their last respects to Jack," laughed Hoghead.

Rooster smiled, looked at me. "And maybe that reincarnation shit's real after all, and Jack done come back as a bird."

"Could be," I smiled back. "You never know. Could be."

Epilogue

Hoghead, the only prisoner in this story who didn't have life without parole, was released from Donaldson prison in 1995, a couple years after Jack died. After returning to his hometown of Birmingham, Hoghead died of an overdose less than a year after his release.

Rooster became a dedicated Christian, had his sentence reduced, made parole and was released in 2005. He returned to Mobile where he became the pastor of a church. Rooster died in Mobile in 2022.

Caveman is alive and still incarcerated at Donaldson prison.

A couple years after Jack died, I discovered meditation, and started a meditation group at Donaldson prison. This led to a self-help course called Houses of Healing, which I facilitated for the next twenty years.

In 2014 my sentence was reduced from life without parole to life with parole. I was granted parole in 2015 and extradited to Mississippi to begin serving my last sentence, fifteen years mandatory. My first book, Spiral, was published in 2020. After serving 43 years, I'll be released on March 4, 2030.

In all fairness, I must say that many prisons, particularly in the south, are beginning to change under more progressive leadership. These new leaders now understand that the old way hasn't worked, and they are slowly changing a badly broken system, a system that in the past repeatedly released illiterate, angry, and wounded prisoners back into society. They understand that what we need are treatment centers staffed by well-paid, well-trained professionals who understand the complexities of human behavior and how to effectively treat mental illness - men and women who are passionate in their resolve to help offenders heal and are willing to help guide them to lasting change.

These new leaders understand that prisoners aren't animals, and shouldn't be treated as such; that they aren't just black-and-white squiggles in a book of statistics, or strangers in some faraway land; they are your neighbors, although you may not know them, and your mothers and fathers and sisters and brothers, although you may not acknowledge them. Sure, prisoners have made mistakes, sometimes horrendous ones (and a few convicted felons may never be rehabilitated, and should therefore be supervised their entire lives), but all prisoners are living, breathing human beings, and most just like you, have their own hopes and dreams and imperfections.

Most often it's not what is done to prisoners that is so harmful, but rather what is not done for them.

R. Troy Bridges
South Mississippi Correctional Institution
July, 2024

Afterword

My thanks to Peggy King for encouraging me to include illustrations in this book. I also thank her daughter and grandson, (my publishers and friends), Ruth Porter and Robby Porter for their years of support.

Special thanks goes to Amy Spungen for her advice and editorial guidance.

I thank South Mississippi Correctional Institution Superintendent Brand Huffman and Business Manager Amanda Huffman for allowing me freedom of expression, no small gift in prison.

Most of all, I thank Jacqueline Dicie, my loving wife, for all her years of love, encouragement, and support.

R. Troy Bridges
South Mississippi Correctional Institution
July, 2024

About the Author

R. Troy Bridges has spent over forty years in several of America's most infamous prisons. In 1993, while in an isolation cell, he had an epiphany that led to a complete change in perspective. This revelation was later written as the short story, "*Another Gold Nugget*", and published in the best-selling, Chicken Soup for the Prisoner's Soul.

In 1994, he started a meditation group in the maximum-security prison, Donaldson, and later, with the help and support of the Lionheart Foundation, facilitated a self-help course based on the book, Houses of Healing. Over the next ten years, he taught hundreds of prisoners how to meditate.

In 1998, he was interviewed in Susan Skog's book, *Radical Acts of Love*, and that same year featured in the magazine, "*Prison Living*".

He is an award-winning artist, whose work has been favorably reviewed in "*The Boston Globe*". During the almost thirty years he spent in Donaldson Prison, he helped create a faith-based program called the Honor Dorm that became a model for prisons throughout the state of Alabama. He also helped bring to Donaldson a ten-day meditation retreat called Vipassana—the first ever in a maximum-security prison in the United States.

His work as an illustrator and artist for the award-winning prison magazine, "*The Angolite*",

has recently been included in the newly-created
collection of the Smithsonian National Museum of
African-American History and Culture in
Washington, D.C.

This is his second book.

Made in the USA
Monee, IL
29 April 2025

16524494R00125